C.A. Greene

The Tobacco Slave

And how to be liberated from its fetters

C.A. Greene

The Tobacco Slave
And how to be liberated from its fetters

ISBN/EAN: 9783337410445

Printed in Europe, USA, Canada, Australia, Japan

Cover: Foto ©Andreas Hilbeck / pixelio.de

More available books at **www.hansebooks.com**

THE TOBACCO SLAVE

——AND——

How to be Liberated from its Fetters.

———

Its Debasing, Debauching, Killing Power

AS OBSERVED THROUGH A LAPSE OF HALF

A CENTURY, BY

DR. C. A. GREENE,

GRADUATE OF THE BERKSHIRE MEDICAL COLLEGE

OF PITTSFIELD, MASS. OF 1848.

———

MEMBER OF THE NEW ENGLAND HISTORICAL SOCIE-
TY, AND THE ASSOCIATION OF THE OLD
HAWES SCHOOL BOYS, AND OF THE
BOSTONIAN SOCIETY, AND THE
PILGRIM SOCIETY OF
PLYMOUTH,
MASS.

BOSTON, MASS. 1889.

P. L. Schriftgiesser & Co., Printers, Boston.

INTRODUCTORY.

During the last fifty years, I have been collecting, collating and condensing articles from every conceivable source on the above subjects, intending sometime to place them before the people in the interest of humanity. Only a portion of this collection is embodied in the within work, and I now throw this little volume before the reading public, knowing that it is illy put together, confessing that my professional duties alone occupy all my time and gives me no opportunity (had I the ability), to make a perfect work.

I do not make any pretentions to being a bookmaker. No profession (on my part) to use eloquent oratorical or finished sentences. The whole desire is, in so arranging my conceptions and the experiences of others in a plain, impressive, axiomatic way, so no one can read them without being wholly satisfied with the truthfulness of my conclusions.

PREFACE AND PREDICTION.

In order to settle the two questions of "Does tobacco in any and every form in which it is consumed
injure mankind?" and "Can you determine by looking at a man who uses it (either as snuff, or in the
form of cigars, cigarettes, or who chews it), how
much it has affected, perniciously, his body?" I
wrote out on the 16th of June, 1886, six names of
some of the most prominent men in the city of Harrisburg, Pa. (where my offices were then located as
a practitioner of medicine), who would die within a
year from the poisonous effects of nicotine. All of
the men mentioned were, at the time of the above
writing, attending to their various avocations.
Mr. Wilson, Mayor of Harrisburg, Daniel Eppley,
president of the Farmers' Bank, A. Fahnstock,
John Shoemaker, ex-Mayor Boas and ex-Mayor
Herman composed the group of names. Three of
them died within the year, two of them in 1887, viz:
May 23, Mr. Boas, and November 14, Mr. Fahnstock, and John Shoemaker in the spring of 1889.
He stopped the use of tobacco in 1886, which pro-
longed his life. Gen. Grant in the same manner
extended his life long enough to finish his memoirs.

I am more than extremely anxious to set this volume afloat amid the untold and uncounted styles of literature in our land, hoping it may become so popular and so well-known that the victims may become aware of the vicinity of the "hole of the cocatrice," and the alarming proximity to the various diseases within described, and the premature deaths that follow; and that the rising generations of America may let tobacco severely alone. I am fully and advisedly aware of the terrifying facts that millions of my race are slowly and regularly sapping the strength, life and vitality of their systems, and that tobacco is steadily producing more diseased bodies and more deaths than from the use of all intoxicants combined. If the Prohibition party is composed of true philanthropists, they will at once investigate the startling statements herein made, and attach "No tobacco" to their anti-liquor platform; and in their crusade against rum and gin, fight with equal valor the other arch enemy of mankind,—*nicotine.*

If there is no combined action of the intelligent men and women of our country against its use, we shall in a few years degenerate physically, mentally and religiously into a heathenish condition.

Being extremely desirous of doing what is in my power to stop the further advancment of the nicotine maelstrom which is devastating our fair country, and to thwart the machinations of the devil, or some other evil genius who is trying to saturate the systems of Americans with the subtle, insiduous poison of this filthy, death-dealing weed, and to throw all the information possible before the growers of, and dealers in the nasty tasting herb, and to raise the greatest obstacles within my reach to its continuance from a philanthropic stand-point, has caused the issue of the within brochure, which is devoted and dedicated to the innumerable victims of nicotine throughout Christendom.

ESPECIAL NOTICE.

Agents wanted in every town, village and city in the United States to sell this book.

Extraordinary inducements offered. For particulars, address the Author.

INDEX.

9

TOBACCO

Its Kindred Companions.

—o—

A BOUT 1831 I signed an anti-rum, and anti-tobacco pledge in Joy Fairchild's Church in South
Boston, Mass. and the year before a temperance
pledge in the Sunday School of the Park Street
Church, on the corner of Park and Tremont
Streets of the same city. A few years afterward
my beloved teacher of the Hawes School, South
Boston, (viz. Joseph Harrington) instituted an
anti-swearing society, probably the first of its
kind in the United States, and its beneficient effects
spread like wild fire among the boys, and it soon
became unpopular to use an oath in that portion
of the city. So great was the alteration in the character and actions of the boys, so influenced by a
good determination to get rid of a bad habit, that
the citizens noticed the marked moral change.

The never to be forgotton philanthropist Hon.
Amos Lawrence, in riding through this suburb discovered the absence of profanity, and calling up one
of the boys and learning the cause, he sent his check
for $100 to Mr. Harrington to be given to them
to be used for any purpose for their enjoyment.
The members of the Society spent it in purchasing
a nucleus of the first library in Hawes School. My
name does not appear among the original members
of the Society. The boys said sometimes I would,
when excited, contract darn it into dam it, and hence
I was on the probation seat for some thirty days
when my name was placed upon the book as an
anti-swearer.

As a sign at a cross road indicates always the
way to a certain town, so these pledges have
ever been kept before my memory and always
acted as barriers to any inclination to break either
of them. Like guardian angels they have appeared at any hour of temptation. And as human nature is much alike the world over, I would
(had I the opportunity) present similar pledges to
every member of the human family. I was then
only a boy, ready to be warped out of shape, or
kept in a correct manner of living, and as we know
that "As the twig is bent so is the tree inclined."
So we must know that an early settlement of these
all important questions is best for all the children
in the universe. Our first impressions are usually
lasting, and, hence the great need of producing
good ones. From the above date I have been a

constant witness to the numerous ills, crimes, etc.
produced from the use of intoxicants and tobacco,
and could I print all my collection of experiences
upon the above subjects they would make a vast
volume. I have been fondly wishing for many long
years to bring together in concise form the list
of multitudinous ills, crimes, annoyances and diseases produced from the use of tobacco. I have
promised my patients and friends for a quarter of
a century to sometime write out and print a portion of them. And first let me say that since
1842 when I commenced the study of medicine I have
given a deal of attention to this especial subject, and
during all of my years of practice I have never met
with a physician who has devoted much study to
this most important theme. One prominent reason
is that as the use of this weed has become so wide
spread it is unpopular to speak or write against its
use, and physicians as a class, like to sail with the
tide. They rarely take counter positions, and hence
they have not taken up the matter. If any treatise
or book has ever been printed by a physician on
the mal-action of tobacco, I have never seen the
work. Now I am well satisfied that if individuals
and societies do not organize to show its ill effects
to the world, that we shall drift still more rapidly
towards a universal use of it. The rapid strides
it has made in popular favor in my time are appalling.
In 1835 it was illegal to smoke a cigar or pipe in
the streets of Boston, Mass. If such a law was
now enacted and enforced, one quarter of our race

would be imprisoned or fined. If the destruction of tobacco by smoking and chewing increases with the same rapidity during the next half century that it has since 1836 nearly all of the citizens of the world and women and children will become its victims.

Without making any pretense to write the origin and history of this vile product, or the many fruitless attempts to stop its progress by legislative enactments, I propose to bring together in this book statistics and documents collected during the above years, together with my own experiences, as found in my practice, in order to arrest the monster in his death-dealing mission. I *candidly believe that the use of tobacco to-day in the United States is doing more harm and killing more victims than all of the alcoholic stimulants* combined. And I trust my readers will understand that my whole ob‐ ject (in a nutshell) is to lay such an array of startling statistics and facts before them as to cause them to give up its use, if its victims, and to let it alone if they have never tasted its nastiness.

THE SALIVA.

Nature has constructed all parts of our systems in a wonderfully accurate manner; under each ear are two bodies, manufacturers of spit, called the paro‐ tid glands; under the tongue is another called sub‐ lingual. The object of these glands is to make from day to day the saliva necessary to keep the mouth or tongue lubricated, or moistened, and to mix with

the food while being masticated, in order to assist
in digestion. Now the very first chew of tobacco
that enters the mouth, or the first inhalation of
smoke, causes an irritation of these glands and all
portions of the inner part of the mouth, and, in
time, all of the mucous tissues in the nose, and in the
ratio of using the poisonous weed, the inflammation
increases in extent, until it reaches all portions of the
air passages; after a time the inflammation is changed
to the ulceration of the tissues, and they are disin-
tergrated and gradually destroyed, swallowed or
thrown out of the mouth with the saliva. The
glands steadily increase in size, and the secretion
becomes unnatural in quality and is increased in
quantity. Probably five pounds would be a normal
amount to be made and used in a day; habitual
uses of the weed often make four quarts a day.
One of my patients saved and measured the amount
thrown out during the waking hours of one day, and
told me he had ejected from his mouth one gallon.
This would be one hundred and twenty-eight
ounces, and it required at least six pounds of blood
to make this quantity. After a time the inflammation
extends slowly down the windpipe into the lungs,
and death from pneumonia or consumption ends
the suicidal life. I have examined carefully thousands of throats of habitual users of tobacco, and
I find the inflammation in *every throat*. Not a single
exception. The tobacco is a sedative, acts like
opium; so when the throat looks like an old burn,
full of ulcerated spots, and the tongue is full of cross

cuts, and the palate is enlarged and elongated, and
the rear portion of the mouth is full of corruption,
there is usually little or no pain, and hence the victim of this insiduous poison is unaware of the morbid
horrible condition of his throat. His breath becomes very offensive; he is a walking privy, and in
conversation with his companions, they constantly
smell the evidence of this filthy cesspool.

The poisonous effects are noticed in some cases
much more rapidly than others. Some men loose
their taste in a very few years, are affected with
catarrh, loss of hearing, and the vision is injured
by its use. Others seem to use it with impunity
for scores of years. The majority of mankind never
devote any time to the study of physiology, hence,
are not good judge's of their physical condition,
suppose themselves well, when the machinery is
badly out of order, hence when such men say: "I
have used tobacco for years, it does not injure me."
Their assertions are worthless. Of what earthly
use would a man's opinion be concerning the Arctic
ocean, if he had never seen it, heard, or read about it ?
The swallowing of the morbid saliva causes indigestion in thousands of cases, stops the formation of
pure blood, and sooner or later all of the organs of
the body give way to the permeating subtle poison.
The air in rooms of tobacco users becomes rapidly
vitiated to the injury of innocent persons, and his
own lungs are slowly ruined by the inhalation of
the nicotine fumes, mixed with the exhalations of
his putrid throat.

THE TEETH.

Hundreds of times I have been told by some unfortunate, "I was informed that tobacco preserved the teeth, and prevented toothache." I commenced extracting teeth when a student in 1842 and continued it up to 1882, and I say advisedly that millions of teeth are annually ruined by tobacco. The nicotine turns them black. The teeth of all old chewers of the weed, are worn down like the teeth of an old, old horse, who has eaten nothing but whole corn for a lifetime. The crown of the tooth is worn off and the enamel discolored and destroyed. Those who are stupid enough to carry pipes for hours in their mouth wear out ridges in the teeth by this asinine habit. *God never intended a man's mouth as a smoke-hole, or as a recepticle for any fluid or substance that swallowed could not be converted into blood.*

Notwithstanding the fact that there is irritation, inflammation and an altered condition of the mucous membrane of the throat and adjoining parts and they are being constantly injured and diseased by the use of this objectionable vegetable, no matter how it is used, whether as snuff, or smoked or chewed, yet all the organs are constantly fighting against the foe, trying to keep the parts in a normal condition. The recuperative power within us is very, very strong. Unfortunately, the action of the poison of nicotine is of a sedative nature. If the first chew or smoke would kill, then there would be no argument in its favor, but God has so constructed our bodies that we can slowly accustom ourselves to any poison, no matter how virulent, so as to be able to increase the quantity used without killing us.

The inhabitants of Lower Assyria eat arsenic in small quantities. Hundreds of thousands of Chinese, Japanese and Americans eat or smoke opium until a dose that would kill a person unaccustomed to it can be swallowed with comparative impunity. The world is full of persons who, in some way, make a bad use of their mouths. The nicotine sore throat is exceedingly common; in many cases it degenerates into the epithelial cancer, the same as it did in Gen. Grant's. Four years before he died, when he was at Point Comfort, I wrote him and told him that when he began to go down he would do so suddenly; predicted his end, and told him I would gladly break up his habit of smoking and restore his health gratuitously.

Although the nicotine throat looks like an old ulcerated burn, there is little or no pain and disturbance, only an occasional tickling, or a cough, which the uneducated dupe says is a slight cold; "I've taken a slight cold." The inflammation may take years before its descent into the windpipe, and air cells of the lungs is particularly noticeable, then comes the stich in the side, the sharp, quick pain, slight difficulty in respiration; hundreds of cells may look like the unfortunate throat, and yet the imperfect respiration goes on, and the ill effects of nicotine slowly and surely pervades the body, and finally kills the victim. If he dies suddenly, the post mortem declaration is "Death from disease of the heart." More than one-half of all such sudden deaths are caused by tobacco. In 1876 I was practicing in Philadelphia, and Gen. McKibbin, of the Girard House, introduced me to Gen. Imboden, formerly of Richmond, Va. who says "I have had for several years what I call a rupture of the heart. It comes often at night ; I think my heart has burst open. I lie conscious, but cannot move, expecting death every moment. I have consulted the experts of this city, New York, also in London, etc. No one can tell me my condition, or the name of my disease. Will you tell me ? " I answered, " No ; but I think I can cure you." He went under my charge ; I stopped his use of tobacco, and in a few weeks the explosion was gone. He was one of the Commissioners at the Centennial of 1876 on tobacco.

I stop from five hundred to eight hundred persons every year from its use. I cannot cure any affliction of the body, and let the patient continue the use of the weed. I have stopped hundreds who have tried again and again to give up its use, but who lacked the power. Under my methods they have no desire for it in a few days. I remove the nicotine from the system in various ways, and destroy the appetite. I have stopped persons who have used it for sixty years, and who, when well, declare they would not, for any price, resume the habit. It often affects (in a few years) the memory, which usually returns in a few months under Omnipathic treatment. It always affects the kidneys after a few years' use; it sooner or later diseases every organ of the body, more or less, the same as a pound of Assafoetida would, in time, affect all the water in a huge tank, and I have said a thousand times that to merely stop its use is of no particular service. If you should thrust fifty pins into your arm and then stop, would that be enough? If you should throw ten dogs into a well and stop, would that be enough? No; you must take out the pins and dogs; so the nicotine must be removed from all parts of the body, which can be readily done by the Omnipathic meth- ods, and if they afterwards when well introduce even a small piece of tobacco into their mouths, they become fearfully sick.

One-half the cases of Bright's disease in men orig- inate from the use of tobacco. Fine, portly-look- ing men, who can for years withstand the ill effects, all at once show signs of this common affliction.

NOTE—RECAPITULATION.

I anticipate the objection of some reader of this brief volume when he says the author has intro- duced the same ideas several times. I have in some instances done it on purpose to catch the eye, so it would be retained by the reader, and occasionally simply because I cannot spare the time from my medical labors to take out repetitions.

HABITS.

Bad and good habits are readily learned. One as

easily as the other. I take very little stock in the "Man is prone to evil as the sparks are to fly upwards," Men and women usually prefer to do good rather than bad acts. The company one keeps has a deal to do with his life. If surrounded by good people, filled with good intentions, you are very likely to at least imitate them. A pamphlet before me says $85,000,000 was spent in the United States in 1885 on public education; and $600,000,000 on tobacco. Now as you increase the amount spent on educating boys and girls in physiology with especial reference to the ill effects of alcohol and tobacco, in a much larger ratio will the use of stimulants and tobacco decrease. The use of tobacco in other words is caused by a lack of the knowledge of its ill effects. No one will purposely thrust his hands into a coal fire. But with the uneducated on this subject it would be as difficult to prove its injurious effects as it would be to prove that the mouth of the Mississipi is narrower than the mountain rivulets where it has its origin. A boy who hears another say dam it, learns it with great rapidity. Try the experiment and say Mary every time you get excited, and would have sworn, and you will find that Mary comes easily in place of God, or any other oath. Some college boys tried the experiment to see how often they could urinate for three days, and when they stopped they found the constant desire to micturate continued. Millions of men in this country are setting (to the rising generation) the bad habit of smoking, they naturally suppose it is beneficial and right to do it. So the malady increases. Ex-Consul Haldeman told me that Chinese girls only eight years of age carry pockets for their tobacco and pipe. Could anything be more pernicious?

In 1887 I placed the following advertisement in several of the papers of Harrisburg, Pa. A few of the members of the Legislature had died previously, some suddenly, and the Doctors blamed the ventilation as being imperfect. The deaths were nearly all caused by the use of tobacco, and its pernicious effects from being deposited on the carpets, floors, and in the spittoons. Hence the within reference:

NICOTINE.

Diseased throats, induced from chewing or smoking tobacco, are alarmingly common and unfortunately the unhealthy individual is not aware of the chronic inflammation which is slowly sapping the health of the victim. The mouth, throat and windpipe are being saturated with the extract of the weed and the drugs introduced into it by the manufacturer, and they are constantly vitiating, poisoning the air that passes in and out of the lungs just as old dead skunks would pollute the surrounding atmosphere of any locality where suspended. The impure air thus entering the respiratory organs cannot perform properly its functions of oxygenating and revivifying the venous blood, and hence it leaves the lungs and enters the heart and is forced through the body in a bad condition, making poor tissues and a poor body generally. The kidneys make herculean efforts to take off the increasing impurities (the virus of nicotine), and being so overworked they become diseased, and Bright's affection of the Kidney's or diabetes are the results. The lungs are also constantly annoyed, and they become inflamed from the introduction into them of the smoke, carbonized nicotine fumes, ashes and other mephitic odors. The salival glands, which should ordinarily make, say, forty ounces of saliva a day, make when so abused 50 to 100 ounces in 24 hours, drawing constantly on the blood for this purpose. This drain upon the system is sure sooner or later to put the machinery out of order.

No pure air ever enters the lungs of the user of tobacco. A constant fight for supremacy is going on through life, and the whole of the body is sooner or later involved in the trouble thus commenced by making a bad and wrong use of the mouth. I have warned hundreds that they might suddenly die from its ill effects. I told our late Mayor (Wilson) in 1886 that he would not live out the year without he stopped its use. I told Daniel Eppley the same not sixty days before he died suddenly. I have stopped over 2,500 persons from using it in four years; broken up the habit and cured their ill-conditioned bodies. No use to talk of better ventilation in the House of Representatives until they banish the pipes, tobacco and spittoons full of putrescence.

Do you understand? No man ever used tobacco in any form who did not have an inflamed (and after a time) ulcerated sore throat, with usually no pain. The nicotine acts like opium in preventing the pain.

NOTE.

Many persons called upon me after reading the above statements, and desired further information. Many stopped its use. In some cases the farmer who raised it stopped its cultivation.

HUMILIATING.

Millions of men devote the major portion of their lives in triturating tobacco and thus making salival solutions, and then in a *manly* manner expectorate it out on to the carpeted floor, or elsewhere. They are apparently under a strict contract with the growers of the weed to work thus studiously at this loathsome job, as though their very lives depended upon the fulfilment of their oblitions. Look at a set of humans thus destroying tobacco in a smoking car. Funnels ought to be placed in them to spit in and thus let it escape on to the track, instead of making the floors look like a last years pigeon roost.

SORE THROAT.

After anyone has produced the peculiar horrible nicotine throat, I do not believe it would ever get well without assistence even after the stopping of the use of the weed.

Feb. 1st. 1888 Rev. S. C. Swallow of Harrisburg, Pa. placed himself under my charge. On examining his throat I found the ill effects of the weed, and yet he stopped its use twenty-six years before, after using it thirteen years.

TO MALMOUTHERS.

Remember (all ye individuals who pervert the use of liquors and tobacco, who, against the plainest declarations of nature, thrust into your mouths these nauseous defiling substances) that God gave you a head with brains in it, with more intelligence than the brutes that you should not act contrary to His dictates. He stood you upright, with head above the body, containing the senses of sight, smell and taste, that as a watch tower, it would see all shoals and avoid all irregularities. The next time you are ready, with so much ceremony to place a quid of tobacco or a glass of rum in your mouth, take your place opposite a mirror, and request your friends, or your wife and children, if married, to watch the misguided deed. Ask them to listen to your colloquy; then say: This tobacco contains a deadly poison, nicotine. It was terribly hard for me to get my mouth and stomach accustomed to it. They made all the resistance they could, but I forced them to accept it, and have, for several years, continued to use it. I know my mouth tastes horribly, I know my breath is very offensive to you, I am aware that I am gradually undermining my health, that I am a suicide, that I

am spending money that should help to pay my debts
or to give you a better home, clothes, and food, I
know I am setting a bad example to you, my dear
boys and girls. I am quite sure that, as your friend,
I could not ask you to accept me as your archetype,
that I am disobeying the laws of God and the Bible,
that soon I may become a drunkard and a pauper.
I am sure that I, with other just such stupids, am
paying an immense revenue to the rum and tobacco
sellers, I am aware that the gold that gilds their
doors and halls, their costly trappings, bars and
furniture, stately stores on corner lots comes all
out of our pockets, that they are our greatest
enemies, that they destroy the happiness, soul and
life of their victims. I am sure that three-quarters
of all the prisons in our land are filled with criminals, murderers, burglars, thieves and highwaymen
who, through rum, became infamous, and now I've
called you all together to notify you that, as I am
still a reasonable accountable being, I have deter-
mined to say to you that I'll never use tobacco or
any ardent spirits again as long as I am spared to
live, and will try to show others how to avoid these
perversions of manhood, invented by the arch de-
ceiver, that hereafter my mouth shall drink only to
quench thirst, and shall fulfil the requirements of
nature, viz. to eat, breathe, drink proper liquids
and speak with.

The above article was published in 1876 in Philadelphia in a magazine (issued by the author of
this work) entitled "Openeye."

TEMPERANCE SCHEME.

In 1882, I published the within article on temperance. I republish it, hoping some phi-lanthropist will take advantage of my offer. Since its publication and distribution (at my expense) many clergymen have adopted a portion of its suggestions. I gave one to our worthy Baptist Minister, Rev. Mr. Botterill; after reading it, he at once, in real earnest, commenced a temperance movement in his Sabbath School. In 1879 Hon. James Black, of Lancaster, Pa.(who ran for President of the United States on the Prohibition ticket of 1874,)became my patient. He is the real father of that movement in this country. He has one room in his spacious house devoted to temperance litera-ture, and the number of his books are very numer-ous. You will there find any and everything ever published on the subject, and he has spent thou-sands of dollars in trying to make the subject pop-ular. He is unfaltering, and honest in his belief that prohibition is the only way to rid our country of intoxicants. By his request, I delivered two lec-tures in Lancaster in 1879. I was then practicing Omnipathy in Reading, Pa. The Lancaster *Era* printed nearly all of my lecture, which was profusely illustrated. Some weeks after I received a letter from a prominent member of the Total Abstinence Society of Massachusetts, asking my terms, etc. to deliver the same lecture in New England; all of it except the portion which referred to tobacco. He says, "We know of the ill effects of it, but we are only fighting intoxicating liquors." My reply was, "So far during my life, when I tell the truth I try to tell it all; the whole truth for me or none."

A NEW SERIES OF SCHEMES,

Called the "Universal Temperance Combination," by Dr. C. A. Greene, Lancaster Pa.

If Jay Gould or any other millionaire or philanthropist will give me from time to time, as it is needed, the necessary funds, I can and will bring about in Pennsylvania, New York or any other State, in a few years, (comparatively,) an approximation to a general temperance condition of the major portion of its inhabitants. Some of the main features of the platform are as follows:

First. I would engage the services of one hundred moral, energetic temperance men, as many as possible of the Murphy type.

Second. I would establish a temperance newspaper, the contributions of articles to be supplied by the above one hundred men.

Third. I would have Hogarth's Gin Lane and Deacon Giles's Distillery, and the illustrations of the diseased condition of the stomach, brain, kidneys and liver, caused by the use of liquors, of Dr. Sewall's (entitled Pathway of Drunkenness), chromoed in excellent style, large enough to be seen on a wall.

Fourth. I would set the hundred men to work writing and compiling short stories on temperance and intemperance.

Fifth. I would publish, on good substantial paper and binding, the above literature.

Sixth. As soon as the above matter was fully under way, I would have a dozen or more of the one hundred men learn and show in the best manner the drama of Dr. Robinson's Reformed Drunkard, with proper scenic effects.

Seventh. When thus armed and equipped in the strife of temperance vs. intemperance, I would organize the above body of men by the appointment of president, vice-president, secretaries and treasurers.

Eighth. I would send to the shire-town of each county of the State, one of the above corps to commence his temperance work, all of them acting under the same methodical and systematic rules and regulations.

Ninth. The work of the agent would be to distribute into every family a copy of the State newspaper and tracts, giving with the matter the general and detailed intentions of the organized temperance combination, asking co-operation and assistance. The agent will call upon every one of the teachers of the Common and Sunday Schools in every town in the County, as well as upon the clergy. He will commence his work by the distribution of the newspaper and tracts, and a notice to attend one or more lectures upon the above subject. An address on temperance should be delivered in every town as often as once a month. I would have a committee of ungloved men formed by the agent in every town as co-laborers to arrange for meetings and in establishing the temperance organizations, cadets, etc. Let the agents and corps call upon all men, who are addicted to the use of tobacco or ardent spirits, reason with them, give them tracts; let them frequent the highways, by-ways and the hovels of the inebriated and poor.

Each agent will be provided with three pledges. Whenever convenient present the first one, in which the signer agrees, with God's help, to abstain through life from the use of tobacco, opium, or any kind of drink containing alcohol, and not to swear, and to use his example and influence to induce others to do the same.

The second shall be a pledge to abstain from the liquors only. The third to abstain from tobacco and swearing.

These pledges shall be printed in books, and the signature in ink be carefully and orderly inserted in the same with the date attached. When the books are full of names they shall be the property of the local organization wherever made up, and shall be sacredly kept for after reference.

Let the above illustrations, with printed descriptions of the same underneath the engravings, be hung in every day and Sunday school and public hall in the State, on the walls of the academies and colleges, and distributed at cost price or (when possible) gratuitously, in every homestead and place of resort in our land. Let no teacher take charge of a school who is not a teetotaller. Let it be understood by him that he takes upon himself an obligation to aid this reformatory movement, and establish a society of boys and girls who solemnly agree not to swear, use tobacco or ardent spirits during their lives. Let them renew their vows as often as once a month. Let them form debating societies, and as often as once a month meet together for the discussion of these subjects in their various attitudes, conditions, etc. read compositions, sing, and in other ways make the meetings agreeable and entertaining. In these and other methods to be invented by the agents, speakers and editors, let the rising generations and the people all over the State, know the horrors and the iniquities of intemperance, and the beatitudes of sobriety, Persuade and reason; do not attempt to drive or imprison. Have the fullest sympathy with the moderate drinker. Let it be known and understood that the condition of the constantly intemperate man is a diseased one, and he should not be treated as a criminal. He should not be incarcerated with felons, but should be placed in a reformatory establishment. Whenever possible the school commissioner and the superintendent of the Sabbath schools shall be appealed to to assist in carrying out the good work. The agent will forward to all teachers who agree to support the work, other books containing the different pledges, and as often as twice a month he shall publicly offer to receive the signatures of the scholars to the same. The agent shall notify the signers of the various pledges that on the second Tuesday of August in each year, forever, there will be a temperance convention and exhibition of all the organizations in the State, in some city to be designated, with delegates from each county; on which occasion there shall be music and singing of the very best quality, and speeches made and essays read, and declamations and dialogues delivered by the men, boys, girls and ladies, all combined with the exhibition of the play called "The Drunkard." This shall be called the Yearly Jubilee of the Temperance Combination. At the end of the exercises at each yearly meeting there shall be a presentation of money, medals and books, after a plan to be hereafter studied out and perfected, something in this wise: To the largest temperance band in any county of all the counties in the State, there shall be presented $500; to the second largest, $200; to the third largest, $100. To the boy or girl, lady or man, who has as teacher, or in any capacity, obtained the largest combined number of signatures to the pledges throughout the State, will be given a gold medal worth at least $50, on which should be engraved a suitable inscription stating this fact and who were the donors. To the persons who obtained the first, second, third, fourth, fifth, and so on to the fifteenth list, shall be presented with gold and silver medals varying in value, and with suitable explanatory inscriptions on each.

After the August Jubilee I would change the field of each agent; would thus have a new factor in each county. He will on every public occasion ask

contributions of money to be sent to the treasurer
to aid in its usefulness, to make it after a time self-
supporting. He will at the first and all other lectures get from all and every one their signatures to
one of the three pledges.

I would have every signer of a pledge renew his
vow and signature in a book, the first week in January of each year. The drama of the Reformed
Drunkard should be played once a year, free, or at
a nominal charge, say ten cents admission, in every
town in the State, and to expedite matters I would
organize several companies, so as to get over
the territory as soon as possible. In this way and
manner and by the use of new methods which time
and experience dictated. I would keep before the
people, and especially before boys and girls, and
young men and women, the innumerable advan-
tages of sobriety, and the horrible criminal condition of the drunkard. In ten years the boys and
girls who had signed the pledge at the age of eleven
years, would be men and women, and would carry
such weight and influence through the State, as to
have the balance of political power in their hands,
and could easily bring about decided temperance
movements, viz: The closing of open bars for
drinking of what is termed the social glass. The
bar is to nearly all drunkards the starting place in
the road to infamy and death. Every year the
temperance rank of boys and men would in this
manner be geometrically increased. In ten years
temperance men and measures would be so popular

that in the selection of men for all positions and callings of life, where individuals or corporations have the choice, only *such men* would be chosen, from the chief magistrate to the most ordinary official. Many saloons, grog shops and liquor stores would be for rent, and be turned into some other use. Distilleries would become less common, the demon, rum, would be shorn of a portion of his power and an approximation to universal temperance would be reached. If Jay Gould, Vanderbilt, Astor, Cooper or any other philanthropist will furnish me the means, I'll so devote my time and energies as to fully carry out the above attempt at the regeneration of our race. Will commence in the State of New York or any other State in the Union.

When once fully demonstrated in one State, it would be easy to carry it through all others. The Legislature would donate the necessary funds and would greatly profit by it. Every dollar thus invested would save an immense number of dollars, as tramps, paupers and criminals of all classes would decrease in number.

Every inducement is now held forth to the boys. and young men to chew and smoke tobacco and to drink intoxicating liquors, and thereby demoralize them, make them squander their money, destroy their health and ruin their bodies. Some eighteen cigar and liquor stores can be seen in my walk from my office to the Stevens' House in Lancaster, all of them totally useless to mankind as would be so many powder magazines. The above ideas have been occasionally, as a whole or in part, published or made public by the writer since about 1844.

A portion of this same platform (of temperance inducing designs), was presented to a Lancaster audience in 1879.

Among the suggestions then made were the following: There is no subject that should be so continuously thought of and agitated by thinking intellectual men as the one of promoting temperance. Clergymen especially should keep the matter before their congregations at all convenient and proper occasions, and should themselves set a good example. The reverend who puts tobacco in his mouth openly disagrees with the precepts of the bible, which object to a defilement of the mouth: besides he is constantly setting a bad, dirty, expensive, and filthy example to his parishioners, and especially to the rising young and observing girls and boys.

NOTE.

Dr. Greene has for forty years occasionally delivered lectures on temperance; He gave one in the Court House at Lancaster, Pa. in 1881, for the benefit of the Y. M. C. A. By the request of its Secretary, Mr. P.P. Goodman. Also one in 1883 before the Legislature of Pennsylvania.

The above matter entitled "A New Series of Schemes, has been before the public for years in the pamphlet form. To give it a wider publicity it is here inserted anew.

TOBACCO CASES.

In order to give particular cases of diseased persons induced by the use of tobacco, so the readers may see the names and address, and styles of affliction, I will here introduce a few of the many thousands treated successfully.

Professor Treher of the High School of Carlisle, Pa. formerly principal of the High School at Newville, Pa. suffered for nine years with a most aggrevated form of dyspepsia, was greatly reduced in weight, annoyed with headache and other pains, was so discouraged from long doctoring with no improvement that he had almost lost all hope of recovery. On the 4th of April, 1885, he came under my charge, and he at once stopped the use of tobacco, *and gained fifteen pounds in twenty-one days*, and in nine months all his unfavorable symptoms were gone, and he was some fifty pounds heavier, and he then told me he had often tried previously to stop its use without success; and that he would not resume the habit any more than he would put a rattlesnake's head in his mouth.

CORRESPONDENCE WHICH EXPLAINS ITSELF.

SALEM, Pa. Dec. 25, 1885.

MR S. H. TREHER—Dear Sir: Your name and place before the people as an educator is sufficient guarantee of your ability to judge of the merits of Omnipathy as practiced by Dr. Greene, of Harrisburg, Pa. and I wish you would state in a letter to me your own unbiased opinion of what Omni-

pathy may do for a sick man by close and faithful
applications of the remedies as prescribed by him.
I hope you will impute no cheek to me for thus addressing you as a stranger. I write you upon Dr.
Greene's recommendation. Yours Very Truly,

W. R. MILLER.

Note by Dr. G.—In the March number of the
CALL you can see an article entitled, Cancerous
Tumor, removed by Dr. G. from above Mr. Miller's
face. He is the son of Wm. Miller, who was our
representative from Salem in the Legislature of
1884.

REPLY.

CARLISLE, Pa. Dec. 28, 1885.

W. R. MILLER, ESQ.—Dear Sir: Yours of the
26th inst. relative to "Omnipathy," as practiced
by Dr. Greene, of Harrisburg, Pa. is at hand.

In reply, after the manner of the blind man in
Apostolic times who was interrogated respecting
the treatment by which he had been restored to
sight, I will say that I know not what "Omnipathy" may do for others, but as for me, I know
that through its beneficent influence, that whereas
I was sick now I am well.

Less than one year ago, from the effects of mala-
ria and dispepsia of long standing and of an aggrevated form, super-induced by confinement and the
air of the schoolroom which is necessarily always
more or less impure, and from lack of sufficient ex-

ercise, I was reduced to a mere skeleton, height
about 6 feet, weighing about 153 lbs. and I verily believe that I would be in my grave to-day but for
my accidental falling in with Dr. Greene.

· Instead I am now what might properly be de-
nominated a strong, healthy man, and weigh 193
lbs.

My entire physical organism seems to have been
re-created, as it were, and I made a new man.
Life which had become to me well nigh a burden,
is now a pleasure, a veritable existence! I thank
God that such a man as Dr. Greene lives!

It is proper for me to say perhaps that I had
some misgivings as to the merits of "Omnipathy,"
but as I had tried many other physicians of the
Homeopathic and Allopathic schools and had received but little benefit, and that only in the form
of temporary relief, I resolved to try Dr. Greene,
and much to my delight and gratification, I began
at once to improve, and have so continued up to
the present time with the results as before stated.

I have long questioned the propriety of the internal use of drugs in the treatment of disease, believing that all the ills that human flesh is heir to could
be treated most successfully by the external application of the proper remedies.

The body is not unlike a huge sponge, and as
we all know it will absorb readily all poisons
brought in contact with it, causing a derangement
of the functions of the various organs which in turn
cause the physical organism to sicken and die; and
why might not remedials be applied to the surface of
the body by means of the absorption of which diseases could be reached and eradicated from the
system?

Such in brief is Dr. Greene's treatment which he
styles "Omnipathy." An hour's conversation with

the venerable doctor will, I think, convince even the most skeptical that his system is the only real natural one (so far as known) in existence. Believing the treatment to be an entirely rational one, and knowing it to be a simple and effective one, I have no hesitation in recommending "Omnipathy" to any and all who are in any way afflicted.

Hoping that I may at some time be the recipient of a communication from you after testing the merits of "Omnipathy," I remain

Very Respectfully,

S. H. TREHER.

ADDENDA.

On the 8th of May, 1889 Prof. Treher wrote Dr. Greene as follows: "Hoping you are meeting with unbounded success in your efforts to establish a School of Omnipathy I remain

Sincerely Yours,

S. H. T.

ANOTHER.

Feb. 8th, 1886, Mr. David H. Fowhl of William's Grove, Pa came under my charge in a very bad condition, with loss of memory, constipation, dyspepsia, ulcerated sore throat, and tonsils so large as to almost close his throat, all occasioned by the poison of tobacco. He had no appetite, little blood, · very nervous and generally out of order, he had used tobacco for fifteen years, and had frequently tried to stop it without success. He could not overcome the appetite. On the 5th of April he called in to see me and reported himself better in every way, said he stopped the use of tobacco at once, and in a few days all his desire to use it was gone.

ANOTHER.

May 13th, '82. Josiah S. Ebersole of Middletown, Pa. came to me suffering from the poisonous effects of the nicotine of tobacco. He had made many vainless efforts to stop its use, but the unnatural habit was deeply rooted, the pernicious poison had impregnated his whole body, and like a polluted well containing dead cats, the only cure was in removing the noxious substances from his body, as the cats must first be taken from the well before any cleaning would have any beneficial effect. He had without avail tried drugs in his stomach, this was like introducing more cats. He at once stopped the use of tobacco. In a short time he became decidedly better. One day some bees required looking after, they were swarming. Lighting a cigar to keep them away from his head, he started out, supposing he could smoke without any inconvenience, but the effects of the nicotine had been partially removed, and he was greatly astonished to find himself growing dizzy, faint, and the sweat pouring out of his body. The cigar was thrown away, but he was obliged to lay still for some time on the ground. He could not use any more tobacco.

TOBACCO 23 YEARS,

PRODUCING AN ENLARGED HEART.

Mr. William H. Shope, a tailor, of No. 26 South Tenth Street, of Harrisburg, Pa. (works for Mr. Ross,) had an affection of his heart and an ulcerated throat, closely simulating cancer, for many years. In March, 1886 he was laid up an entire week with terrible palpitations of his heart. A prominent physician of this city, who attended upon him told him he could give him relief, but no one could cure him, and he was liable to die any day.

Sometimes he suffered a great deal with pains in his chest and in his throat. He was very nervous. On the 8th of May, 1887, he began using my remedies, and in a letter written me January 6th, 1888, he says: "In four months every vestige of my affection of the heart left me, and my brother who is a physician in Halifax, Pa. examined me and said there was no diseased condition of my heart. Up to the commencement of your treatment my measurement was 34½ inches around the breast, 29½ waist, 35 for the hips. They are now 38 breast, 35½ waist and 39 hips. I then weighed 115 pounds, and now about 140 pounds. I never felt so strong and hearty in my life as now." In other words Mr. Shope is 3½ inches larger over the chest and hence has increased the size of his lungs, since the using of the right (or rational) treatment.

All these afflictions **were** caused by the use of tobacco. He had what is termed a "tobacco heart," (said it turned over), and the peculiar cancerous throat which was the most difficult portion to cure (same as Gen. Grant). Of all the physicians who treated him, none intimated that the nicotine was killing him. Not even his brother, a prominent M. D. who tried to cure him, and finally notified him, "No cures were ever made in such cases."

Mr. Shope now curses the day he ever was induced to use it.

TOBACCO 35 YEARS.

Read this! Read this! Mr. Thomas Warhurst, of No. 9 Lafayette avenue, Brooklyn, N. Y. sent me the following testimonial: "For 15 years I have had Bright's disease of the kidneys, so pronounced by Dr. Bowen, examining physician of the Mutual Life Co. of N. Y. by whom I was rejected on making an application for a policy of Insurance on my life, and many other physicians have told me the same story. For 12 years I have been disfigured with an ulcerated relict of a carbuncle under my left eye, which threatened to become a cancer. For many years I have constantly tried to get cured and have only tested the physicians called most skilful. Two of them were my relatives. I have also tried all the best known patent (so called) medicines with no benefit or even relief from any or all of them. Having been the manager of the celebrated musician Blind Tom, for 20 years, and with him travelled over the civilized world, my opportunities of knowing of physicians reputations has been unequaled, and I have sought far and near for one who could cure me: in vain. On the 16th of October, 1886, while exhibiting Blind Tom in Harrisburg, Pa. I placed myself under the charge of Dr. C. A. Greene, Omnipathist, who treats all diseases of the body by *external applications* of non-poisonous medicines (no drugs internally). His treatment has acted like magic in my case. I am now 60 years of age and a well man, and not a vestige of my kidney disease or the ulcerated carbuncle remains. I will gladly repeat the above evidence and more to any one who will call upon me, or address me by letter. Besides the above afflictions I had an ulcerated sore throat and symptoms of the gout and nasal catarrh, all of which have disappeared. Several members of my family and relations have been cured by Dr. Greene's remedies. My brother-in-law, T. P. Clark, of Bennet, Neb. was given up as dying with chronic diarrhœa and other complaints. Dr. Greene has cured him and never saw him. He is 1,600 miles from his office. I truly admonish all persons who are suffering from any disease to test the novel treatment of Omnipathy and quit swallowing drugs.

Mr. W. had a regular tobacco sore throat; it looked as though previously burned, (just as bad as Gen. Grants), voice would occasionally give out. He kept his son with him in cases of emergency. In April, '87, he wanted to act as my agent in letting the world know more of " Omnipathy."

He established and continued to act as my agent for six months at No. 9 Lafayette Avenue, Brooklyn, N. Y. and through his intervention, I gave four lectures in the Historical Society's rooms, and treated some six hundred patients.

TOBACCO TWENTY YEARS.

CANCER ON THE FACE.—On the 27th of April, 1887, Mr. W. J. Russell came 700 miles to my office, from Fayette, Ohio, and commenced using my remedies for a bad looking CANCER on his face. He had a very inflamed throat and was out of health in several ways. On the 7th of December he writes me: "I am entirely well, in every way. No sign of a cancer on my face." Before coming to me he was often induced to have it removed with a surgeon's knife.

If Omnipathic physicians were as common as allopathic the knife would soon be a useless instru‐ment, and a race of healthy men and women would soon be raised, who, ignoring the use of anything taken into the stomach and mouth that could not be converted into blood, would be a race of strictly temperance people. There would be no use for calomel, opium, quinine, whiskey, tobacco or any prohibition party if it (Omnipathy) was generally adopted. As every one would know that the use of the mouth, stomach and intestines is only to put in food and moisture, such as water, milk, etc. and they make blood, and the blood cures disease and recreates the whole body.

This man had a tobacco sore throat for years, which culminated in the above cancer. The same grounds were gone over with him, the tobacco stopped, etc. He is not only well now (June 5th, 1889), but tries successfully to get similar cases to become my patients.

ECZEMA.

Hundreds of men have skin diseases caused by the use of tobacco. In ninety days after using Omnipathic remedies they usually disappear.

There are many persons suffering from the poison of tobacco who would like to stop the habit and relieve their bodies of the nicotine that has impregnated their tissues and parts; to such persons let me again say that we have stopped thousands who have had the habit so strong as to think it impossible to leave it off. Stopped one in this city who has been using it for forty-five years. He says that his whole life seems changed for the better since he has rid himself of the filthy, unnatural expensive stuff, and that he would not be so enslaved again for $100, and that he has chewed and smoked over a ton of tobacco. I recently stopped a man who had

used it sixty-four years, a man of wealth and influence. He had been told by leading physicians that
it would kill him to stop it. I told him it would
kill him if he did not let it severely alone, and all at
once, and I am happy to say his appetite is gone.
In November, 1888, I told one of my neighbors of
Arlington again and again that he was liable to die
suddenly from its poisonous effect, that he was too
thin, not blood enough, and saturated with nicotine. I told him in January. 1889, the same in my
office in presence of Dr. Kyle's father, of South Boston, and other witnesses, and even offered to treat
him without any charge, and the next Saturday he
died, just one week from the day he was in my office.
The only way to stop its ravages is to send
such works as this broadcast over our country and
introduce into every school in our land a simple
physiology containing proofs of its injurious effects
upon the body.

A prominent man of Brooklyn, N. Y. had his
tongue and a portion of his lower jaw cut off by the
surgeons of his city, for which they charged him
$2,000. He had the same kind of tobacco throat
as Mr. Warhurst, and there was no more benefit to
be derived from their mutilating his body than there
would be to cut off one head of a snake, when he had
twenty more. After so disfiguring him, they saturated him with morphine and kept him unconscious
of his condition. He was (while in bed dying)
placed under my charge, and two months afterwards, at the end of one of my lectures in the His-

torical Society Rooms, he introduced himself to me, thanked me for saving his life, and said he was sixteen pounds heavier than before they so horridly cut off his tongue.

If it would be of any service to the reader, I could give hundreds of similar and dissimilar cases of every variety of disease, from the same cause could issue a huge volume, but they would be after all only repetitions. I might say that the Crown Prince of Germany, who died after repeated mutilations, died from the poison of nicotine. Cases of cancer of the stomach and intestines, men sallow, attenuated cadavarous, unfit for work, with no courage, no push, imperfect memories, almost constant pain in the back, every organ in the body in a mal-condition, with loss of manhood, are all the result of chewing or smoking the unnatural herb.

HOGARTH'S "GIN LANE."

In 1853 I visited the Philadelphia, Pa. Library on Sixth street, and there examined at great length a series of Hogarth's picture. Among a large number of these sketches made by him in 1751, was one entitled "Gin Lane," which, in a remarkably vivid manner, illustrated the innumerable evils of spirit drinking. If old Hogarth was not an anti-gin and anti-tobacco representative, it was not for lack of evidence of their ill effects. I wish I could recall him from the spirit world to aid me in showing all the bad points of the tobacco question.

In "Gin Lane" you have scores of Talmages sermons condensed into vivid illustrations, no end to the variety. S. Gripe's sign is over one man's door. The kindred signs of pawn brokers, dealers in old clothing, tobacco, whiskey, ales, gin and beers, are seen everywhere. Every kind of diseased humans are represented taking in saws, kettles, pots, clothes and other articles of personal property to the pawn broker, to obtain money to buy ardent spirits and tobacco. A drunken man and a dog are eating meat from the same bone. Another sign says "Drunk for a penny, dead drunk for two pence, and straw thrown in." A lazurite looking woman, with her bosom exposed, is in a beastly state of intoxication on the top step of a house, half holding a shrieking child, which is falling over a banister; on a lower step is the just alive skeleton of a man, holding a card inscribed "The downfall of mad gin." In the distance are jails, poor houses, insane asylums and prisons. In the background may be seen a dead inebriate about to be coffined. A child, thrust through the abdomen by a huge fork, is held up to view by the drunken father; on the right a sign, "Ready made coffins." You see through a broken hole in the wall of a dilapidated building, in an upper chamber, the representation of suspended respiration viz. A drunken man hanging by a rope. On a board is "Killman, wholesale distiller." Cripples and unfortunates of all kinds and hues are portrayed in every conceivable form and a drunken prostitute is being wheeled somewhere in a barrow, while another female is forcing some

rum down the throat of an innocent child. You
will also read the following verses:

FIRST.

Gin, cursed fiend, with fury fraught,
  Makes of human race a prey.
It enters by a deadly draught,
  And steals their life away.

SECOND.

Damned cups that on vital's prey,
  That liquid fire contains,
Which madness to the heart conveys,
  And rolls it through the veins.

THIRD.

Virtue and truth driven to despair,
  Its rage compels to fly,
But cherishes with hellish care,
  Theft, murder and perjury.

TOBACCO IN 1764.

In a copy of Nathaniel Ames Almanac for 1764,
(now in my possession) appears the following article on tobacco. "The incomparable Dr. Boerhave
says that when the saliva is lavishing by being spit
away, we then remove one of the strongest causes
of hunger and digestion; the chyle prepared without this fluid is not of so good a condition, and the
blood is worse for being deprived of this diluting
liquor."

SMOKING CARS IN THE REAR.

The magnates who control the making up of trains, do a great injury to the lovers of pure air by placing the smoker's in front of any passenger car, they only punish the innocent by compelling them to re-breathe the vitiated air of the misguided men and boys who occupy the other.

The Directors make a great mistake in the inhumanitarian act of furnishing well appointed cars to be occupied by men so misdirected in their manners and habits as not to be able to forgo the use of the pernicious habit, while riding from one locality to another.

ALBUMS AS BRIBES.

Every inducement is offered to get men, girls and women to use up the weed in the multitudinous forms in which it appears. Every variety of wood and material are used for pipes, pipe stems, or holders. One firm in New York offers a fine album to any cigarette smoker who brings them a quantity of tags, to indicate the number of cigarettes destroyed, and this firm say they have given away 250 albums in a day.

While engaged in one vicious business of inducing men and boys to use the vile weed in chewing. smoking and snuffing, the sellers go further. They place pretty girls faces on the boxes and also women's nude forms, thereby increasing the men's immorality. The clergymen have noticed this devilish action in their pulpits, and yet it is done openly and boldly so men may be more rapidly prostituted. This satanic sword cuts both ways in demoralizing men, and they demoralize women. And the most astounding phenomena and remarkable coincidence in the world is the fact that with all the attempts of bad, evil-disposed men. combined they have never succeeded in inducing the American women, only in a few instances, to use in any form this devilish shrub. Thanks to the virtue and intelligence of the American women. In contradistinction let me quote from a daily paper the following:

A curious custom that attracts the attention of strangers in Panama is the spectacle of native women walking along the streets smoking long, slender cigars. It is the habit of the women there to gather in the public markets as early as sunrise to gossip and talk over their affairs while enjoying their morning smoke. Their confabs take the place of a newspaper.

A BRIEFE & ACCURATE TREATISE,

CONCERNING THE TAKING OF THE FUME OF TOBACCO,

Which Very Many, in These Dayes, doe too

Licenciously Use, by

TO. VENNER, OF LONDON,

Doctor of Physick in Bathe, 1637.

In which the immoderate, irregular and unseasonable use thereof is reprehended, and the true nature and best manner of using it, perspicuously demonstrated.

The hearb Tobacco is of much antiquitie and reputation among the Indians of America. It is also
called Nicotian.

The above article is the title page to a work on
the subject of tobacco. Read it, and you will see
that its evil effects were known in 1637.

HISTORY OF TOBACCO.

John Nicot introduced tobacco into France in
1560. He was an ambassador of France at the
Court of Lisbon. In 1585 it arrived in England,
through Sir Francis Drake, from Tobago, one of
the windward groups of the West India Islands.
In 1624 snuff taking became so odious that Pope
Urban excommunicated all persons found using it
in the churches. In 1634 the Russians made a law
that all snuff-takers, upon conviction, should have
the nose cut off, but soon after, discovering the
frightful commoness of persons bereft of this appendage, the law was repealed. In 1653 the council of
the Canton of the Apponzell in Switzerland severely
punished all persons found smoking. In 1719 the
Senate of Strasburgh prohibited its cultivation. In
1565 an apothecary of Augsburg, Germany, received dried tobacco leaves from France as a new
drug. In the course of the seventeenth century a
number of books on tobacco were published in
Switzerland and Germany. In Italy, the clergy became protectors of the Satanic herb. Bishop Tornaboni sent the first seed of the plant from
Paris to Florence. To Rome, the seed was first

sent by Cardinal de Santa Croce (of the Holy Cross)
Papal nuncio at Lisbon, and after him the plant
was named the herb of the holy cross. But at Rome
tobacco first met opposition. Pope Urban VIII,
(because laymen and clergymen were snuffing during
divine service), excommunicated snuffers in 1625.

In Spain, at the convent of San Jago de Compos-
tella, famous for pilgramages, five monks were im-
mured alive in 1692 because they had smoked at
the choir in the evening. Yet Pope Benedict XIII,
himself a passionate snuffer, allowed the use of tobacco again in 1724. Secular governments, too,
opposed the use of tobacco. King James I. of England wrote a lengthy essay in Latin against it in
1603. The University of Oxford held a public dis-
putation against the smoking of tobacco in 1605.
In France only druggists were allowed to sell tobacco
when prescribed by physicians. In Sweden, at the
time of Gustavus Adolphus, smokers had to do
penance in the church. In Russia smokers were
unmercifully whipped, while their noses were torn
open in 1634. About the same time Sultan Murad
IV. went around in Constantinople during the night
time, accompanied by executioners, who killed those
he discovered smoking.

In Persia, soldiers found smoking were killed, and
their smashed hands and feet were thrown · before
their tents. Also among the Mohammedans the
clergy were bitterly opposed to the use of tobacco.
In Germany, where the first smoking of tobacco
was chronicled in 1620, the authorities waged war

against its use (after the thirty years' war), from
1618 to 1648, was over. The city council of Berne,
Switzerland, ordained in 1661, that smoking of
tobacco should receive the same punishment as
adultery. But all the opposition was of no avail.
Tobacco remained victor. Thereupon the government commenced to tax it. The Republic of Venice
first did this in 1657. It decreed the sale and manufacture of tobacco to be a monopoly of the State,
leased the same and derived a net income of 46,000
ducats from it during the first five years. This example was at once followed by the papal government at Rome, and in a short time by the governments of all the other States in Italy. In France,
Colbert, the prime minister, made a similar ar-
rangement in 1674, and the goverment of France
derived from the sale and manufacture of tobacco
a revenue of five hundred thousand livres in that
year, which rose to 29,000,000 livres during the
year 1687. In England also a tobacco monopoly
of the State was established, but it lasted only
about twenty years, when it was abolished, giving
way to a tax on tobacco. In all civilized countries
of Europe tobacco was heavily taxed in the seventeenth and eighteenth centuries. The tobacco plant
is now extensively raised in Europe, and manufactured there into snuff, smoking and chewing
tobacco, all of which are taxed as luxuries. As to
the production of tobacco, the Gartenlaube says:
The annual amount of it raised at present is, in
the United States, 3,400,000 hundred weight;

Cuba 610,000; Brazil, 300,000; India, 150,000; Austria, 100,000; the Netherlands, 85,000; Italy, 93,000; Russia, 180,000, and Germany, 1,100,000.

Of the several States of the latter country Prussia produces, in round numbers, 230,000 hundred weight; Baden, 242,000; Bavaria, 156,000; Alsace-Lorraine, 160,000, and Hessia, 31,000. The tobacco raised on the whole earth amounts to about 13,000,000 hundred weight annually. The present annual consumption of tobacco per head of the total population is in Russia, 1 pound; Italy, 1 1-2 pounds; Cuba, 2 1-5 pounds; Austria, 3 2-5 United States and Germany, each 3 pounds; Belgium, 5 4-5 pounds, and Holland, 5 3-5 pounds. Tobacco, in the shape of snuff, smoking and chewing, although in itself not a very attractive thing, has millions of devotees all over the world.

ITS ORIGIN.

Tobacco was discovered in San Domingo in 1496; afterwards by the Spaniards in Yucatan, in 1520. It was introduced into France in 1560, and England in 1583.

AMOUNT OF TOBACCO CONSUMED.

"Everybody smokes in Siam—men, women and children," said Mr. John R. Halderman the returned minister from Bangkok, Siam, to a reporter.

The above was cut out of the *Washington Post.*

STARTLING STATEMENT.

The rapid increase of tobacco manufactured in this country is worth noting. Last year 3,457,309,-017 cigars and 994,334,000 cigarettes were made in the United States alone, requiring over 91,000 pounds of leaf. In 1872, not 40,000 pounds were used. The vast bulk of tobacco, however, is consumed in " other manufactuers," which required 217,451,000 pounds in 1884.

That the reader may have a slight aproximate idea of the magnitude of the above quantity of tobacco let me give you a little arithmetic. Supposing each cigar was 4½ inches long, and each cigarette was 2½ inches long, and they were all laid down end to end, the cigars would extend 1,296,-940, 875 feet, and the cigarettes would reach 165,-722,333 feet and together would make 1,452.213,-208 feet or 276,934 miles. In other words they would wind around the world more than eleven times. In this insidious manner are the millions of men, women, girls, and boys, using up this immense amount of filthy weed, but the lamented part beside the vast expenditure of money, and time lost in lighting matches, and smoking the weed is that every one is injuring the body that God gave him charge of. Still there are thousands so saturated with the virus of this plant and so opinionated in its favor that you might with as much propriety expect to extinguish a huge fire by expectorating upon it human saliva, as to convince them of its baneful effects.

The number of cigars sold on Broadway, New York, is estimated at 20,000 daily. Of these, one-twentieth part cost 30 cents, one-fifth 25 cents, one-fifth 20 cents, two-fifths 15 cents and and three-twentieths 10 cents. Thus Broadway spends upon its cigars $3,300 per day, or $2,050,850 per year.

It is estimated that in the city of New York 75,-
000,000 cigars are consumed yearly, the total cost
of which is $9,650,000. Add to this the amount an-
nually expended for pipes and tobacco, and we
have an aggregate of ten and a half millions as
New York's yearly account with retailers of the
weed,   The 75,000,000 cigars, if laid end to end,
would extend one and a half times across the At-
lantic, or, if laid side by side, would build quite a
wall of cigars from New York to Albany!

In the manufacture of the article there are 946
firms engaged. These firms are (in so many instances)
unworthy of credit that the government, in order
to secure the fulfilment of the provisions of the law,
require   of them penal bonds. which at present
amount to $7,947,000,   There are some four thous-
and machines, such as cutters, presses, snuff-mills,
etc.   The State which has the most manufactories
of the filth is North Carolina, the number being
191; Virginia follows, with 178. The number of
persons engaged in manufacturing cigars is 10,827,
and they give bonds in the sum of $21,374,000.
The minimum of a cigar manufacturer's bond is
$500, with an additional sum of $100 for every
registered cigar-maker employed. Of these, New
York has 2,896; Pennsylvania, 2,543; Illinois,
553; Maryland, 327.

The gratification of our depraved appetites costs
a far larger sum than would support all our poor-
houses, feed and cloth our poor, fill the treasuries
of our great Christian missionary societies and

carry on all our schemes of education. It is a little thing, seemingly, but the aggregate is fearful to contemplate.

We have pauper families, (it has been ascertained), which have spent more than a thousand dollars on Tobacco, counting principal and interest. We have genteel clerks who spend annually from one to five hundred dollars on cigars! We have a chief magistrate who, on a late back trip from Boston to New York, with his suite, smoked a hundred dollars worth of cigars! Who pays this bill? Do Boston gentlemen pay it, or the State of Massachusetts? Can we reverence a smoking volcano as chief magistrate?

In 1880 Germany destroyed by smoking 650,-000,000 of cigars, and 60,000 tons of tobacco were used in pipes, and 8000 tons in snuff, and 700 tons for chewing purposes.

U. S. CENSUS FOR 1879.

General Walker Superintendent of the U. S. Census for 1879 says. "There are 638,841 acres of land in the U. S. on which 472,661,159 pounds of tobacco was raised, which when worked up into all the various kinds of cigars, plugs, etc. would probably sell for $500,000,000.

—The consumption of tobacco in France during the past five years has averaged 53,000 tons, thrice the consumption in 1832.

—Forty-eight million pounds of tobacco are annually consumed in Virginia's 172 tobacco factories.

— The English duty on tobacco amounts to some $45,000,000 a year.

— The greatest snuff taking country in the world is France, though it shows a decline in the habit. In 1869 the consumption was 13,000,000 pounds, or seven ounces per head. Now it is five ounces.

— In southern Russia and the Caucasus the women smoke almost as universally as the men. A newspaper correspondent writes: "I have had, two or three times, nicely dressed ladies step up to me in a railroad station or on the platform and beg of me a light."

— Over 16,000,000 pounds of tobacco have been sold in Lynchburg, Virginia, since October 1, 1881, an increase of 700,000 pounds on the scales of the previous tobacco year.

— One estimate is that $610,000,000 worth was used up in 1887. In order to give some idea of the vastness of this amount, suppose it was silver dollars in a huge pile, and a man could count one a minute or sixty an hour and replace them in another heap, and would continue so to do for ten hours each day It would take him 3,511 years to get through with the operation, and he would have lifted during these years 38,126,000 pounds or 19,063 tons of silver. If the tobacco was made into strips five feet long and one pound to each strip, and one inch wide, it would make 192,500 miles and reach eight times around our earth. It would make a bridge over Philadelphia, from the Delaware to the Schuylkill River one and one-half miles wide.

—During 1887 there were made in this country 3,177,860,952 cigars, about forty for every pound of tobacco used. About 35,000,000 were imported, thus making a total of about 3,150,000,000, or sixty for every man, woman, and child in the United States, and 250 for every man over 21 years of age.

—We are a nation of Smokers and chewers. The sales of leaf tobacco at Lynchburg, Va. in one week aggregated 1,243,000 pounds. The sales for the season of 1887 aggregate 25,200 pounds over the same months of 1886.

—New York is the centre of the cigar-making trade. She has nearly 4,000 factories and turns out 1,000,000,000 cigars a year. Pennsylvania, Ohio and Illinois rank after New York.

THE VOICE.

Mr. Lennox Browne, an English physiologist, finds that drinking and smoking affect the vocal organs. Statistics furnished by no less than three hundred and eighty professional vocalists have shown him that a singer should avoid all stimulants.

—158,539,468 pounds of tobacco were raised in Kentucky during the year 1883.

NATIONS USING TOBACCO.

A statistical comparison showing the relative extent to which various nations are addicted to the use of tobacco has been published by the *Etoile Belge*, which manifests no little pride in the position occupied by Belgium. The proportions are:

For England, France and Russia, 5; for Italy, 7;
for Cuba, 11; for Austria, 14; for Germany and
North America, 15; for Belgium, 24; and for Holland, 28. In some parts of the New World, however, the achievements of the Dutch are, according
to the same authority, altogether surpassed. The
readers of the *Etoile Belge* are informed that in
Mexico everyone is, with very rare exceptions, a
smoker. The school children who have done best
in their studies are rewarded by being allowed to
smoke a cigar as they stand or sit at their lessons.
The schoolmaster himself is seldom without a cigar
in his mouth. In the law courts all persons commonly enjoy their tobacco freely, and even the accused in a criminal trial is not denied this indulgence, but is allowed, if his cigarette goes out in the
heat of the argument, to light it again by borrowing that of the policeman who stands at his side
to guard him.

Cut from Boston paper of Jan. 24, 1888.

Straiton & Storm made last year 42,659,589
Cigars, a greater number than any other manufacturer by more than FIFTEEN MILLIONS. No
better evidence can be given to show their immense
popularity. The sole New England distributing
Agents for these fine Cigars are Wait & Bond, 53
Blackstone street, Boston.

In 1888 the United States manufactured 14,000
000 pounds of tobacco, 400,000 pounds of snuff,
4,000,000,000 cigars, and 1,500,000,000 cigarettes.

INCONSISTENCY.

Some people talk a great deal about ministers and the cost of keeping them, paying their house rent, table expenses, other items and salary. Did such croakers ever think that it cost $35,000,-000 to pay the salary of American lawyers; that $12,000,000 are paid out annually to keep our criminals, and $10,000,000 to keep the dogs in the midst of us alive, while only $6,000,000 are spent annually to sustain the thousands of preachers in the United States? These are truths, and statistics will show them to be facts. What one thing exerts such a mighty influence in keeping the republic from falling to pieces and the nation from becoming like Sodom and Gomorrah, as the Bible and Ministers? Skeptic — croaker — tell us ?

ITS USE IN MEXICO.

Out of 7000 stores in the city of Mexico, 1072 of them sell tobacco in some form, and 1184 sell pulque and liquors.

TWO BILLION CIGARETTES A YEAR.

Recent enterprising methods of advertising causes this enormous increase in business. According to statistics compiled from the records of the internal revenue department, more than 2,000,000,000 cigarettes were sold in the United States during the year 1887. If the remainder of the present year fulfils the promise of the first six months the record of the year 1888 will exceed that of the previous twelvemonth.

"If the cigarettes are as injurious as they are claimed by those who declaim against them," said a well known manufacturer to a reporter for the Mail and Express, "It would seem that this community at least, ought to go down to an early grave. Of course anything that I might say would necessarily be said from a prejudiced standpoint, and it would be useless for me to attempt to argue the matter, and I am willing to let the popularity of cigarette making speak for itself."

There is no doubt that the widespread use of cigarettes has been due to the extraordinary methods which the manufacturers have adopted in order to advertise their separate brands and thus bring them before a too willing public. It is safe to say that in no other business has the art of advertising been more satisfactorily conducted as to the advertisers themselves or more popularly so for the public.

In the United States there are practically less than a half-dozen firms that control the entire cigarette business, while the product of all the rest combined is scarcely worthy of notice. The representative of one of the principal firms was interviewed by the reporter to ascertain some facts relative to methods which the manufacturers have of advertising their wares and the experience of the firm called upon is, to all intents and purposes, that of the others.

The most popular way of advertising cigarettes at present, is by the insertion of a slip in each package, which tells the purchaser that on the presentation of a certain number of similar slips at the office of the company a beautiful album containing useful and artistic pictures of designs will be given free of cost. In this way the manufacturer easily gets valuable information as to the class of people patronizing his goods, while the purchaser himself is well satisfied.

If the statement of the reporter's informant is to be believed there is one firm in this city which gives away every day no less than 250 of these albums, 30 of which are distributed in the city daily, while the remainder are sent through the mail to all parts of the country. While explaining the history of picture-giving by these manufacturers, which began a few years ago, the speaker handed the reporter a copy of the particular album published by the firm. It was indeed a work of art, in its way, being a pamphlet of the heaviest paper and containing 48 pages, including the cover, and each page was filled with colored representations of the coat-of-arms and flags of all the nations of the world and of every State and Territory of the United States. Were it not that the conspicuous advertisement of the firm which issues it is displayed too prominently, the work would be an ornamental as it certainly is a useful adjunct to the library. The mechanical art displayed in the books is of the highest class, and the illuminated pictures within its covers are handsomely mounted.

"Of course it costs us a great deal of money to

prepare and publish a work of such a nature." said the firm's representative, "but it pays us well on the whole, even though it diminishes our profits to a large extent. It is a personal satisfaction to me to distribute the albums to those who call for them. Sometimes the rush is so great during the hours we have set for distribution that we hold quite a levee. The majority of those who bring the requisite number of slips are young men who evidently have saved them from boxes purchased for their own consumption, but a great many of the callers are boys, and girls, who have kept the slips which their fathers or brothers have discarded.

TOBACCO COUGH.

This is a very common afflction, but in most cases, the cough is only occasional. Hence, it does not attract the attention of the victim as being of any consequence. It is usually a short quick one, as though the throat was temporily obstructed. If asked why do you cough? the reply is "I have taken a little cold."

THE POX, OR SYPHILIS.

I have seen several cases of chancre of the lips among smokers. Many such cases are on record, caused by using a borrowed pipe, or by the wrappers of the cigars being moistened by the saliva of a syphilitic cigar-maker.

You might as well attempt to carry a hot stove in your naked arms without injury, as to handle this noxious weed with impunity.

SMOKING AND HEART DISEASE.

In a recent report by Dr. Frantzel, of Berlin, on immoderate smoking and its effects upon the heart, it is stated that the latter show themselves chiefly by rapid, irregular palpitations of the heart, short breath; languor, sleeplessness, &c. Dr. Frantzel says that if the causes of these complaints are inquired into, it is generally found that the patients are great smokers.

THE PRINCE AND HIS PIPE.

[*From the Pall Mall Gazette.*]

There are many anecdotes concerning the love of the German Crown Prince for his p'pe. The Hamburg *Fremdenblatt* adds a new one, which is now obtained "From a source worthy of credit. It is both new and true," adds that journal, "and throws a clear light on the oft-praised amiability and *bonhomie* of "our Fritz.'" The present manager of the Hamburg Stadt Theatre was formerly manager of the Berlin National Theatre, and he is known to have sacrificed a considerable fortune to his ideal-national aims as a guide and leader of the drama in Germany. At that period the Crown Prince was a constant attendant, it used to be said "A demonstrative attendant," at Herr Buchholtz's theatre. The manager, for the special convenience of the Prince, caused a little antechamber to be constructed next to his box, to which he could retire between the acts. One evening Herr Buchholtz entered his little cabinet, according to his custom, to give the Prince a loyal greeting. He observed that his patron, with a sudden action, thrust something behind his back, but in an instant afterwards drew it forth again, exhibiting with a smile a burning cigarette. "You will betray me, Buchholtz," says he. "Smoking, as the notice board says, is prohibited in the theatre." "But your Imperial Highness," expostulated the manager, "this is your private sitting-room." "That is all one," retorted the Prince; "I claim no privilege. You have the right to denounce me to the police. I see only one way of escape—you must be *particeps criminis*." So saying the Prince handed his cigarette case to the manager. Herr Buchholtz bowed, took a cigarette and stuck it in his vest pocket. "If Your Imperial Highness will allow me," said he, "I will keep it as a memento." "Ah!" replied the Prince, "you will escape yourself and betray me. You must take a second and light it." The manager obeyed and the Prince said, "Now you are a fellow-criminal!" This happened long before the fire at Ring Theatre, at a time when the prohibition of smoking was not very strictly carried out, when there was not a little smoking among the actors themselves, according to the narrator.

NOTE.

The Crown Prince died in 1888 from tobacco-poisoning.

BACTERIA IN SNUFF.

A Berlin physician, Dr. Ernest Flothow, was consulted by a patient who was troubled by severe headaches. The physician's inquiries revealed the fact that the patient had been using snuff immoderately. The snuff box was produced, and a microscopic investigation showed that it was swarming with bacteria, which appeared in the form of a fine whitish powder. These parasites, it is stated, bore into the walls of the nasal cavity, where they multiply rapidly and finally find their way to the brain. —*Chicago Times.*

PARALYSIS.

A young man in Chicago, last summer, suddenly found that one side of his face was ailing. An hour or two afterwards his right eye refused to close, and the paralysis of his whole facial region was complete. He went to the doctor and found that personage treating three other young men for exactly the same affection. The right eye remained open four weeks. The sense of taste was greatly weakened. The main nerve, which had been shut off by a decrease in the orifice of the skull, was finally closed, and no chronic effect beyond a slight optical weakness followed in any of the four. It would be interesting to know, adds the *Current*, whether or not tobacco had aught to do with these remarkable cases.

HORRID BUSINESS.

Two ragged Italian children, who were arrested in Chicago while gathering cigar stumps on the streets, explained that they sold the discarded weeds to a fellow-countryman for 15 cents a pound, and that they were "made into cigarettes."

PERSONS MAKING TOBACCO.

Employes in tobacco factories are subject to headache, fainting, gastralgia, muscular spasms and nervous coughs caused by breathing the atmosphere containing the tobacco dust. Dr. Franzel, of Berlin, says that immoderate smoking may appear to produce no unfortunate effect for many years, when all at once, the heart becomes seriously deranged in its action—the result of a sort of cumulative effect of the drug.

CIGARETTES.

If ever the habit of cigarette smoking has thoroughly and permanently fastened itself upon any man, that man is Robert Louis Stevenson, the popular romancer. During one hour of conversation (on his brief visit to New York recently,) an average sized bundle of cigarettes was entirely consumed by the novelist in rapid succession. Mr. Stevenson has ruined his health by the practice, and both of his lungs have been impaired beyond medical skill solely by the constant inhaling of the deadly smoke. He is frankly conscious of the evil effects of the vice that has so insidiously con-

quered him, and despite the most earnest efforts of
his mother, wife and friends, the practice goes on
unabated. With Mr. Stevenson a cigarette is his
last companion on retiring at night, and the first
sought by him on rising. Physicians of all lands
have warned him in vain, fearing the culminating
effects on a constitution already nearly shattered,
and on a mind from which has emanated those
wonderful romances that have made their author
so widely popular in English reading lands.

Hattie Ketchum, the five-year-old daughter of a
farmer and tobacco-grower near Weedsport, N. Y.
is said to be hopelessly addicted to the use of tobacco, and has been since she was two years old.
When between one and two years of age the girl
was afflicted with colic, and at the suggestion of a
friend tobacco smoke was blown into milk and
given her. This remedy proved effective, but crea-
ted an uncontrollable desire for tobacco, and by
various subterfuges the child has ever since found
means to satisfy her cravings for the weed.

CANCER.

Men who must smoke tobacco will do so without regard to the dreadful fate which overtook
Senator Ben Hill and General Grant. The cigarette slave, who inhales and fills his lungs with the
fiery smoke; the cigar devotee, who masticates one
end as the other burns, and the lover of the short
black pipe are all deaf to the voice of warning against
excessive indulgence. The other day a young man,

the son of a college professor, died in his room from heart disease, superinduced by the cigarette habit. The pipe is responsible for many a malignant ulcer that has disfigured the victim for life. Cuban and Chinese workmen who make our imported cigars use saliva to moisten the paste that fastens the end of the wrapper, and who knows what malignant and nameless disorders may thus be propagated? The almost universal diffusion of a taste for smoking has not been accompanied by a knowledge or due appreciation of the evils of excess. Yet these are multiform, palpable and serious, and unfortunately the last extreme horror, which now confronts General Grant. — *Record.*

JUVENILE SMOKERS.

A British physician, observing the large number of boys under fifteen years of age on the street with pipes and cigars in their mouths, was prompted to examine the breath of this class of smokers, and for that purpose selected thirty-eight boys between the ages of nine and fifteen. In twenty-two of these cases he found various disorders of the circulation with indigestion, palpitation of the heart, and more or less marked taste for strong drink. In twelve there was frequent bleeding of the nose, and twelve had slight ulceration of the mouth. The doctor treated them for their ailments, but with little effect till the habit of smoking was discontinued, when health and strength were soon restored.

A medical expert in France, who had been study

ing the effects of smoking, finds that out of eighty-one great smokers twenty-three exhibited an intermittent pulse, independent of any cardiac lesion; and this intermittency disappeared on the smoking habit being abandoned. The effects of smoking on children from nine to fifteen years of age show not only palpitation and intermittent pulse, but chloro-anæmia.

It is asserted that Senator Ben H. Hill's cancer was caused by nicotine, absorbed into a blister on his tongue while he was smoking.

EXPENSIVE.

Thurlow Weed estimates (in his autobiography) that during the fifty-four years he used tobacco he smoked and gave away at least 80,000 cigars.

One Davenport (Iowa) cigar manufacturer employs over two hundred persons and turns out about 600,000 per month.

BRAIN-POISONING BY NICOTINE.

A peculiar case of mental hallucination has just appeared at Battle Creek, Michigan, in the person of a young man about eighteen or twenty years old. He is a cigar-maker by trade, and has been in the habit of smoking from ten to thirty "green" cigars daily. He had not drank liquor sufficient to produce delirium, and yet he is a raving lunatic, and suffers all the horrible phantasmagoria that pertain to the fully developed tremens. He has worked in and used tobacco ever since early boyhood. Of late years he has used it extensively, principally in strong cigars, and it is supposed that the nicotine has so poisoned and shattered his mind as to partly paralize it, thus producing the disorder. He has been taken to the insane asylum at Kalamazoo for treatment.

A SWISS IDEA.

A correspondent from Switzerland writes: "In all the cafes and beer-gardens in Germany may be seen, in the centre of the room, a metal box, placed on a table, which has an opening in the top, into which are thrown the stumps of cigars. These boxes are put there by a benevolent society, with a notice requesting gentlemen to deposit their cigar ends for the benefit of the poor. Every morning an agent of the society unlocks and empties the casket and with what result? At Christmas time in the year 1881 seventeen hundred and twenty-six children were clothed by the proceeds of the sale of this tobacco."

BAD HABITS.

It's a funny old world anyhow, and taste is only a matter of education. Your baby contentedly gums candy, the native African picaninny is joyous over a mouthful of salt, and the young Esquiman cries for a tallow candle; we gorge ourselves on oysters, while the Digger Indian would not give you one long fat snake for all the oysters in Chesapeake Bay. We, or at least you, chew tobacco, the

Hindoo lime, and the unostentatious and not over-fastidious Patagonian, when he wants a chew of something real good, rolls a quid of guano into his cheek.—That's the kind of a gum-drop he is; and you couldn't hire him to chaw tobacco.—Unless, indeed he may have learned the habit from the missionaries.

THE TOBACCO HABIT.

The universal "hankering."—Growth of the cigar business.—Open air treatment. The tobacco habit is one of the forms of stimulation which seem to be common to the crudest as well as the most accomplished beings. Something in man impels him to be happier.

The rude Mexican pounds the century-plant till he can get fermentation in it, and then he drinks himself drunk. The methodical Chinaman who has a duty for every day in the year, and saves his money better than a miser, had the citadel of his nature stormed by opium, and against the command of his government and his religion, he sits down and smokes himself into stupefaction. The Turk, precluded from liquor by his religion, tortures himself between the harem and the pipe. The English beer drinker comes to a place where malt and hops will no longer satisfy, and he must drug his beer to make it palatable, and the public house which he frequents obliges him in that respect by opening the bung-hole and dropping in tobacco or pepper or something sufficiently pungent.

Nothing is more remarkable in the United States than the growth of the cigar business. Before the rebellion, Havana manufactured the best and probably the most of our cigars. After the duties were made high the cigar-making business was transfered within our revenue jurisdiction, first to Key West, and then to New York. The war itself was provocative of the smoking habit as it multiplied the excitement and left hundreds of thousands of men in tents waiting for battle, and there they smoked because they had no other form of enjoyment. So the growth of tobacco was introduced into our northern states, and now the north raises the best smoking tobacco for cigars, and the tobacco interest in some of the western states, amounts to millions per annum. There are said to be 60,000 persons in New York rolling cigars or stripping the leaf. In almost every little village there are cigar factories.

BAD HABIT.

A portland, Me. woman became such a slave to the habit of eating cloves that from taking one occasionally she came to consume a quarter of a pound in a single day. At last she was attacked with all the symptoms of virulent poisoning, and the doctors had a hard struggle to save her life.

Two gentlemen of Norwich, Conn. have had a match at cribbage together nearly every day since Jan. 1, 1882, playing in that time nearly 15,000 games. One of them is now twenty games ahead of the other, and at no time has either had the advantage by more than fifty games.

[*Boston Globe May 26, 1889.*]

We have received not a few letters commenting upon the almost universal masculine habit of spitting. One correspondent has favored us with an account of an experience in a New York horse car, we wish all tobacco chewers and spitters in the country would profit thereby. He designates his communication "Our National Habit."

There were five of them; three on the opposite of the car and two on my side; all were uncomfortably near, and each man was industriously occupied in decorating the floor of the vehicle with discharges of saliva. Three were tobacco chewers, and their copious coffee-colored expectorations soon made unsavory pools at their feet; the other two discharged a white saliva which was only a little less copious and nauseating than the other variety. So persistent and so zealous were these five men in this occupation, that it looked as if they might have been hired to sit there and spit at so much an hour.

My cheeks tingled at first with indignation, but presently the whole thing began to impress me as amusing. Were not these men simply exercising their natural privilege of expectorating where and as much as they pleased? They paid their fare; and a car is a public vehicle in which everybody is as good as anybody else; and what is the floor, anyway, but something to tread and spit upon? Their reply to any protest I might have made would have been advice energetically expressed, to the effect that if I didn't like their doings I might get out and walk or hire a coach. To tell them that they were making the car floor very nasty, and that everybody who came in would have to tread in the filth; that women's skirts would fall into it; that the right their fares gave them was to travel in the car, and not to soil it at their pleasure — to have told them all this would have excited their amazement and their ire. The right to spit was to them as natural as the right to breathe — they had never doubted it, and had never heard it questioned — and yet they were not people of the lowest class. They were dressed tolerably well, and considered themselves, no doubt, respected citizens. But how did these respectable citizens abide in their own houses? Did they cover the floors of the passages, the stairways, the dining-room, the parlor, with stains that the most insensible would scarcely call ornamental? Did they and their wives and their daughters always sit down with their feet in a pool of tobacco juice? And then did they spit all day long as persistently and energetically as they were doing on this occasion? I dared not think of their homes, or follow them in their vocations—to see and hear them for a duration of ten minutes was more than enough.

And yet I was amused. I had just been reading one of Frederick Harrison's brilliant essays on the

"Worship of Humanity"—the new religion which makes mankind the object of worship and reverence, and I thought of humanity, with a big H, as a universal tobacco chewer, as an embodied expression of expectoration and of worshipping it! The picture seemed a little grotesque, and irreverent laughter sprang to my lips.

I am afraid that the thought of a man as a spitter, a chewer of tobacco, as a being carelessly ejecting unsavory streams from his mouth, is fatal to not a few visions of the race. "How noble in reason," exclaims Hamlet, "in form and moving how expressive and admirable, in action how like an angel, in apprehension, how like a god!—the beauty of the world, the paragon of animals!" This is very noble, but in order to sympathize with it fully I must forget my five paragon tobacco spitters in a New York street car; and Hamlet lived before the days of tobacco. "In apprehension how like a god!"—that is, when he seizes upon his tobacco pouch!" "In action how like an angel!"—that is, when he squirts his tobacco juice over your newly polished boots.

In truth, vile habits like tobacco chewing and spitting, kill not only virtue in those who indulge in them, but in those who are compelled to witness them. Who can be inspired to serve humanity when humanity is unsavory and disgusting in its practices? To die for your country is an old patriotic aspiration. Dying for your country is dying for other people; and if other people means my five companions in the street car, with their quids and their ejections, I shall think about it twice.

This habit is altogether American — not merely the habit of tobacco chewing, but the habit among men who do not chew tobacco of ceaseless spitting. The climate is the cause, some say. But American women do not spit more than the women of other countries, and therefore climate cannot be the cause, for climate is no respecter of sexes. We of America are a nation of spitters, and are recognized as such the world over. It is not an agreeable reputation. The spittoon is almost an unknown article elsewhere; here it is a fairly national emblem. In many parts of the country its presence is most revolting. I recall an instance of an artist who was asked to go on a sketching tour in certain districts, and who refused because he would not travel where in hotel and car he must be brought in constant contact with the spittoon and the spitter.

"Love thy neighbor as thyself," is the scriptural injunction. With all my heart, with one mental reservation. He must not be a chewer of tobacco.

WASTED TIME.

Millions of hours are lost every day in the United States, by chewers and smokers of tobacco, in the various attitudes assumed of scratching a match, or the lighting of a cigar, or in arranging the weed for chewing; also in adjusting and readjusting the cigar or pipe in the mouth, or in the dilectable pastime of knocking off the accumulated ashes with the little finger, which to be well done requires education, how to be adroit and not burn the appendage.

YELLOW MOUSTACHE.

Some chewers of the noxious weed wear a stiff bristly style of moustache, tinted with the yellow of the nicotine, and they spend hours of time in fruitless efforts to curl the hirsute appendage.

HYGIENE IN SCHOOLS.

In 1854, by the request of some of the citizens of Philadelphia who had attended my physiological lectures, and also by the solicition of one Von Herringen, who had invented a new musical notation. I spoke for an hour to the Board of Controllers of the Public Schools on the necessity of introducing Hygiene, (with special reference to ardent spirits and tobacco), and music into the above schools. Now twenty-five of the thirty-eight states of the Union use physiological books, and music is common everywhere.

PHYSIOLOGY AND HYGIENE IN THE PUBLIC SCHOOLS.

From the Laws of Pennsylvania made in 1886. An act relating to the study of physiology and hygiene in the public schools of the Commonwealth and all educational institutions receiving aid from the State.

Section 1. Be it enacted by the Senate and House of Representatives of the Commonwealth of Pennsylvania, in General Assembly met, and it is hereby enacted by the authority of the same, that physiology and hygiene (which shall in each division of the subject so pursued include special reference to the effects of alcoholic drinks, stimulants and narcotics upon the human system), shall be included in the branches of study now required by law to be taught in the common schools, and be introduced and studied as a regular branch by all pupils in all departments of the public schools of the Commonwealth, and in all educational institutions supported wholly or in part by money from the same.

Section 2. It shall be the duty of county, city, borough superintendents and boards of all educational institutions, receiving aid from the Commonwealth, to report to the Superintendent of Public Instruction any failure or neglect on the part of boards of school directors, boards of school controllers, boards of education and boards of all educational institutions receiving aid from the Commonwealth, to make proper provision in any and all of the schools or districts under their jurisdiction for instruction in physiology and hygiene, which in each division of the subject so pursued gives special reference to the effects of alcoholic drinks, stimulants and narcotics upon the human system, as required by this act, and such failures on the part of directors, controllers, boards of education and boards of educational institutions receiving money from the Commonwealth thus reported, or satisfactorily proven, shall be deemed sufficient cause for withholding the warrant for

State appropriation of school money to which such district or educational institution would otherwise be entitled.

Section 3. No certificate shall be granted any person to teach in the public schools of the State, or in any of the educational institutions receiving money from the Commonwealth, after the first Monday of June, Anno Domini one thousand eight hundred and eighty-six who has not passed a satisfactory examination in physiology and hygiene with special reference to the effects of alcoholic drinks, stimulants and narcotics upon the human system.

Section 4. All laws or parts of laws inconsistent with the provisions of this Act are hereby repealed.

SCHOOL CHILDREN.

There are 16,000,000 school children in the United States, 10,000,000 of whom are enrolled in the public schools.

Great Britain has now 10,000 Sunday school temperance organizations, with more than 10,000,000 members.

CIGARETTE PAPER.

"There are three kinds of paper used in making cigarettes. They are made from cotton and linen rags and from rice straw. Cotton paper is made chiefly in Trieste, Austria, and the linen and rice paper in Paris. The first, manufactured from the filthy scrapings of ragpickers, is bought in large quantities by the manufacturers, who turn it into pulp and subject it to a bleaching process to make it presentable. The lime and other substances used in bleaching, have a very harmful influence upon the membranes of the throat and nose. Cotton paper is so cheap that a thousand cigarettes can be wrapped at a cost of only two cents. Rice paper is rather expensive. Tobacconized paper is manufactured. It is a common paper saturated with tobacco in such a way as to imitate the veins of the tobacco leaf very neatly. It is used in making all-tobacco cigarettes. Arsenical preparations are also used in bleaching cigarette papers, and oil of creosote is produced naturally as a consequence of combustion. This is very injurious to the throat and lungs and is said to accelerate the development of consumption in any one predisposed to the disease."— *Mail and Express.*

BURMESE CUSTOMS. IDEAL LOVE MAKING AND SIM-
PLE MARRIAGE CEREMONIES. AN INVETER-
ATE HABIT WITH MEN, WOMEN
AND CHILDREN.

I bought two cigars to-day of a woman in the bazaar, writes Frank G. Carpenter from Rangoon, Burmah. They are each a foot long, and one looks for all the world like a poorly developed ear of corn with the husk on. They are very mild, and have little tobacco in them, being made of owher leaves in connection with the tobacco. All of the Burmese people smoke—men women and children. I have not yet seen any babies leave the breast for a whiff of a cigarette, (as the books on Burmah state they do), but I see many three and four year old children smoking, and the Burmese maiden learns to smoke as soon as she can walk. All of the girls are adepts in rolling cheroots, and in Burmese courting, the girl gives her lover cheroots rolled with her own hands and the two take, I doubt not, whiffs about in the smoking of them. It is common to pass the cigar from one friend to another, and in a group of three girls, whom I watched having their fortunes told under the shadow of the great golden pagoda, I saw that one cigar did for a trio.

PHYSIOLOGICAL ITEMS. HOW TO KNOW THE PRESENCE OF IMPURE AIR.

It is estimated that the air in a room becomes distinctly bad for health when its carbonic acid exceeds 1 part in 1,000. An apparatus has been recently patented by Professor Wolpert, of Nurnberg, which affords a measure of the carbonic acid present. From a vessel containing a red liquid (soda-solution with phenolphthalein) there comes every 100 seconds (through a siphon-arrangement), a red drop which trickles down a prepared white thread about a foot and a half long. Behind the thread is a scale beginning with "pure air" (up to 0.7 per 1,000) at the bottom, and ending above with "extremely bad" (4 to 7 per 1,000 and more). In pure air the drop continues red down to the bottom, but it loses its color by the action of carbonic acid, and the more there is of that gas present, the sooner it shows the impurity.

EMUNCTORIES, OR PORES.

It is calculated that there is no less than twenty-eight miles of this tubing on the surface of the human body, and that, on an average, from two to three pounds of water daily reach the surface through these channels, and are evaporated. It is supposed that at least one hundred grains of effete nitrogenous matter are daily thrown off from the skin.

NOT SWEATING.

There is a boy in Putnam county, Tenn. a son of Jefferson Lee, ten years of age, who, owing to the peculiar nature of his skin, has never been known to sweat a drop of perspiration in his life. Another phenomenal feature connected with the boy is that he has only four teeth, and he had these when born, having neither cut nor shed any since his birth. He is very much affected by the seasons. In the summer he gets exceedingly warm, and is compelled, in order to live at all, to keep his head and body wet with cold water, and falls off to almost a skeleton, but when winter comes, and cold weather sets in, he is enabled to dispense with his bath and grows fat. He is said to be a sprightly boy, with plenty of sense.

DRUGS IN TOBACCO.

BALTIMORE, July 22.—The establishment of J. S. Young & Son, for the preparation of bark extracts used in the manufacture of tobacco, at Dranmead's wharf, Corton, was burned last night. Loss, $225,000; fully insured.

OPIUM SMOKING AND OPIUM EATING.

The Great Increase of the Curse in the United States.—Whole Families Being Ruined.—To persons unacquainted with the facts in the case, the figures that are recorded of the amount of opium and morphine smoked and used and the number of opium habitues in the United States to-day would look like pure fiction. Last year over 92,000 pounds of opium were used in this country, but 36,000 of which was for medicinal purposes. A canvass of the drug stores and facts in the possession of opium experts reveal, at the lowest estimate, 57,000 opium takers, of which 17,600 are opium smokers (not Chinese, but American.) Again, 96,700 hypodermic syringes, (for injecting morphine,) were manufactured and sold last year.

When we consider that the large majority of opium eaters were made such by the carelessness of physicians who prescribed this drug without proper precautions, it shows up the medical profession in no very enviable light.

REDUCTION IN SIZE.

When Europeans first visited New Zealand, they

found in the native Maoris the most finely developed and powerful men of any of the tribes inhabiting the islands on the Pacific. Since the introduction of tobacco, for which the Maoris developed a passionate liking, they have from this cause alone, it is said, become decimated in numbers, and at the same time reduced in stature and in physical well-being so as to be an altogether inferior type of men.

If temperance societies would suggest an antidote against hunger, filth, and foul air, gin palaces would be numbered among the things that were.

[Sketches by Boz.

Virtuous Belgium leads the world in tippling. The 5,000,000 inhabitants of that little country annually consume about 60,000,000 quarts of alcoholic liquors. There is an average of one public house for every twelve adult Belgians, and in some parts of the country the supply is nearly twice as great.

Illinois has over 3,000,000 people and 11,000 liquor saloons—an average of 272 to each saloon.

There are 8,000,000 tobacco seeds in a pound.

THE SABBATH.

The commandment Keep the Sabbath Day Holy emenated from God himself, and without any reference to this divine law, let me say as a physician, every working man who uses up either the vitality of his body or brain during the six days of labor, needs one day of rest for recuperation, and he cannot revitalize his body while engaged in selling rum or tobacco, or while pouring ardent spirits into his stomach, or making his mouth a receptacle for this devilish weed. Some of our street corners where men do congregate, look like last year's pigeons' roost, so full of nastiness. The filthy deposits from ulcerated cancerous throats are constant nuisances to all well bred persons. Ladies are especially annoyed while passing these filth depositories, fearing their skirts will be contaminated by contact, or some of the victims to this terrible habit will expectorate (unintentionally) a mouthful of filth upon their dresses. It is a source of rest and is of decided benefit (physically) for anyone to attend a church service. It rests the body and improves the intellect, no matter how debased through any pernicious habits. The Sabbath breakers hence are incapacitated from doing a good day's work on Monday. The frequenters of saloons or shops where tobacco is sold, slowly and surely drift into gambling in some way or another, and soon become proficient in swearing, and thus take the initiatory steps towards worse crimes. Go into any village, or city, of any state or territory of our vast union, and listen at the doors of these venders of malodorous substances and you will hear the unfortunately common oaths: "God damn you."

If a celestial from the interior of China should visit our cities for the first time, he would soon come to the conclusion that every effort was being made and that the great aim of Americans was studiously and regularly to keep their stomach and intestines full of alchoholic stimulants, and their mouths stuffed with tobacco.   If the efforts are only continued, and no one rises up to stop this suicidal career of our people, it will be only a matter of time when our girls, boys, women and men will be engulfed in this terrible maelstrom.

Physicians, lawyers and clergymen are all setting the bad example of using tobacco, and if the educated indicate that their mission of life is to perform such filthy work, certainly the rank and file will follow the ill-timed example.

Seven-eights of every county in Pennsylvania is represented by farmers who grow tobacco. $300 an acre has been paid in Lancaster county for land to grow this weed, and in due time our other crops will woefully decrease as the demand increases for this satanic growth. Spittoons will be found in all our domiciles, schools, stores, offices, halls and churches, and sudden deaths from the ill effects of the poisonous weeds will be as common as flowers in mid-summer.

After my half century's experience of the baneful effects of this potent poison, seen daily without requiring any effort for the investigation, I say advisedly, (with the ability, if required to make an array of thousands of cases of injury to health by its use, not only of the mouth, but of every organ of the body) that the very first introduction of it into the mouth of anyone, does harm as soon as it enters, which is plainly perceptible to any critical, honest seeker after truth, and the evil effects are slowly and insiduously making their marks upon the unfortunate who thus stupefies himself by this unnatural use of the mouth. The tobacco cough is common all over the world. Listen to it and you will soon recognize it. Something in the throat seems, just for a minute, to strangle; then a short, quick, convulsive cough, which only occasionally manifests itself, increased in frequency as the throat becomes more inflamed. Premature death is sure to come to all such victims. Of the thousands who die suddenly (drop while at their homes, shops or in their beds, or in the streets), the vast majority are users of this narcotic in some form. It stops the beating of the heart.

EARLY TRAINING.

Let me again repeat the axiom: There is no safer or more intelligent way in the world than to start with your boys and girls as soon as they fully comprehend anything and teach them the ill results to the body, life and soul from the use of intoxicants, hasheesh, opium, cocoaine and tobacco, and the uselessness and wickedness of using oaths. First impressions, whether right or wrong, good or bad, are very apt to be indelibly impressed upon the mind, and will influence your actions through life.

My father kept a tavern when I was born and my first memory is of events that happened in the immense bar-room at Batavia, N. Y. with its huge fireplace and the big andirons, and bigger burning logs on them. My honorable sire, about the time of my first appearance, discontinued the use of tobacco and stimulants himself and threw them out of his house, and became an advocate for temperance. In this manner my mind was, in infancy, imbued with right impressions. My father, besides giving up the sale of above intoxicants, devoted a room in his hotel to temperance publications, was one of the trustees and built the First Presbyterian Church, and up to his death lived a life consistent with this platform.

[From the *Independent* of 1887].

"It is just twenty-three years ago to-day since I was mustered out of the Bucktail regiment at Camp Curtain," said Joseph H. Meck, foreman of the CALL office, to another old printer, who recalled the fact, for Meck began to work on the *Evening Telegraph* after he left the army, June 11, 1864. Mr. Meck was in fourteen battles and skirmishes without receiving a wound, and of 1,600 men, of which the regiment was composed, only twenty-one escaped uninjured. Mr. Meck is one of these twenty-one and is now in full health and spirits, a veteran who could even yet stand the brunt of battle with a shooting-stick that carries death in its muzzle."

I cut the above article out to impress everyone

with the fact that notwithstanding this man escaped injury during the rebellion, he was the exception to the general rule. So you will occasionally find a man who has used tobacco to old age, but thousands who started with him have died prematurly.

TAKEN TO PHILADELPHIA.

The remains of the ex-Alderman Geiger, of the Auditor General's Department, were taken to Philadelphia to-day in charge of Resident Clerk Chas. E. Voorhees. Mr. Geiger was a member of the Union Republican Club, and was prominent in Republican politics for twenty-eight years. The funeral will take place to-morrow.

[From *Call*, Sept. 29, 1887].

Mr. Geiger died in the Capitol building suddenly, Sept. 28th without any warning. He was an habitual user of tobacco.

ARTIFICIAL APPETITE.

Out of the thousands of persons with whom I have conversed who were using tobacco, I never knew of a single instance where the desire for it was not induced by frequent attempts to chew or smoke it. The majority are sickened, and often vomit when first it is placed in the mouth. There is in man a natural disinclination to use it.

HOW QUICK IT KILLS.

Chambers's Encyclopedia says death has taken place from injections of tobacco into the rectum.

GOOD POSITION.

In September, 1886, The Lutheran Synod met at Gettysburg, Pa. and passed the following resolution:

"Resolved, That this Synod will not hereafter receive nor retain as a beneficiary any young man who indulges in tobacco in any form."

ANTI CHRISTIAN.

Methodist conferences in Wisconsin have declared their belief that Christian men ought not to raise or sell tobacco. Thirty thousand acres of the plant were under cultivation in the state, and much comment has been aroused.

HABITS.

To further prove how easily we imitate or follow bad or good examples, let me say that in 1718 coffee was first introduced into the West Indies. It then began to ·spread through North America and in 1880 over three hundred and twenty-three millions of pounds were consumed in the United States alone.

EFFECTS OF SMOKING.

Malachi Regan, a gentleman fifty years of age, who resides at Steelton, Pa. had a cancer tumor cut from the left side of his lower lip at the City Hospital yesterday. He has always been a great smoker and about ten years ago noticed a small formation on the lower lip where his pipe rested. This has been growing rapidly from the irritation given it by his pipe, and it became necessary to have it cut out.

NICOTINE.

A·physician calls attention to the fact that if tobacco smoke be instantly ejected from the mouth and throat before descending into the chest and be made to pass through a cambric handkerchief drawn tightly across the open lips, a permanent deep yellow stain, corresponding in size and shape to the opening between the lips, and having numerous spots of a darker hue pervading it, will be left on the handkerchief.

DR. HITCHCOCK.

A violent hater of tobacco is Dr. Hitchcock, the Professor of Athletics at Amherst College. He attributes to its immoderate use, (especially by immature young men,) all sorts of physical and mental ailments, and predicts that a quarter of a century more of excess will produce a generation of weaklings.

ACTION OF TOBACCO.

Dr. Treitaski has made a number of observations upon the effects produced on the temperature and pulse by smoking. He found that in every case, varying according to the condition of the individual there was an acceleration of the pulse rate and a slight elevation of the temperature. If the average temperature of non-smokers was represented by 1,000, that of moderate smokers would be 1,008, and while the heart in the former case was making 1,000 pulsations, in the latter it would beat 1,008 times. It is in the latter effect that he thinks the danger of tobacco-smoking is manifested.—*Journal de Medcine de Bruxelles.*

DEATH OF SIRO DELMONICO.

Another of the Delmonicos is dead. Siro Delmonico, one of the famous caterers of New York, died suddenly at his residence Tuesday morning, aged 57. Siro, like his brother whose death took place a few weeks ago, fell a victim to the effects of excessive smoking. He had been poisoned by nicotine. It is one thing to smoke in moderation, or even to what is ordinarily known as excess. It is quite another to use the weed like the departed caterer. His cigars were made to order, so that they might have the desired strength, and he had one in his mouth all the time. A better illustration of the potential strength of the tobacco habit could hardly be imagined.

A GIRL'S PASSION FOR TOBACCO.

[*From the Norwich, (N. Y.) Telegraph.*]

. A girl about twelve years of age is frequently seen on our streets, and is truly an object to excite pity. She is poorly clad, and sometimes wears an old blanket over her head, but more frequently is bareheaded. Her passion is tobacco. She smokes continuously. She enters our groceries and asks for pipe and tobacco. If she obtains the weed she is perfectly happy. Whatever intellect she ever had seems muddled by her uncontrolled habit. Her face is pale and her eyes heavy and dull. Our youthful cigarette smokers should take a good look at this unfortunate girl. It might lead them to restrain their appetite for the deadly nicotine.

ITS ILL EFFECTS.

Here is a boy who has never used tobacco.

"Charley, will you help us to try an experiment?"

"I will, sir."

"Here is a piece of plug tobacco as large as a pea. Put it in your mouth and chew it. Don't let one drop go down your throat, but spit every drop of juice into the spittoon. Keep on chewing, spitting, chewing, spitting."

Before he is done triturating that little piece of bacco, simply squeezing the juice out of it without swallowing a drop, he will lie there on the platform in a cold, death-like perspiration. Put your finger on his wrist. There is no pulse. He will seem for two or three hours to be dying.

Again: steep a plug of tobacco in a quart of water, and bathe the neck and back of a calf troubled

with vermin. You will kill the vermin, but if not
very careful you will kill the calf, too.

These experiments show that tobacco in its ordinary state is an extremely powerful poison.

BAD BREATH.

May never lady press his lips,
  His proffered love returning,
Who makes a furnace of his mouth,
  And keeps its chimney burning.

May each true woman shun his sight
  For fear his fumes might choke her,
And none but those who smoke themselves
  Have kisses for a smoker.

CONCERNING THE HABIT OF SMOKING.

Several reasons have been assigned for growing
tobacco in England. One that should have been
obvious, however, has been overlooked. Either
smoking must he encouraged by making the loathsome plant a native of the soil, or England as a
smoking country will soon be nowhere. The people
who have never been able to see the justice of allowing others a cigar when they do not smoke
themselves, will learn with surprise that the average Belgian smokes four times as much as the average Englishman.   There are five hundred and fifty
pounds of tobacco consumed in Belgium for every
one hundred inhabitants. Holland, Germany and
Austria come next, and France stands seventh. Of
all the European countries, England very nearly

smokes least. Spain, which is the lowest on the list, averages over one pound per head, and England's average is only one hundred and thirty-eight pounds per one hundred inhabitants. If Spain did not fritter away its time over cigarettes, England would be the country that smokes the least in Europe.— *St. James' Gazette.*

MEXICAN HABITS.

In Mexico nearly every one is a smoker. The school children who have done well in their studies are rewarded by being allowed to smoke a cigar as they stand or sit at their lessons. The schoolmaster is seldom without a cigar in his mouth. In the law courts, all persons commonly enjoy their tobacco freely, and even the accused in a criminal trial is not denied this indulgence, but is allowed, if his cigarette goes out in the heat of the argument, to light it again by borrowing that of the officer who stands at his side to guard him.

NO SMOKERS.

Right here to give you a breath of good air, and to let you know that there are men of intelligence who have never used the filthy weed, let me introduce

HABITS OF SUCCESSFUL MEN.

Of the men in New York who can justly make some claim to success in this life, the following do not drink, smoke or chew: Chauncey Mitchell Depew, Jay Gould, Russell Sage, Cyrus W. Field,

Henry Clews, Stephen Van Cullen White, Commodore Arthur Egerton Bateman, Collector Magone, Washington E. Connor, Alexander E. Orr, John D. Slayback and Pat Sheedy.

Dr. O. S. Taylor of Auburn, N. Y. was born Dec. 17, 1784, and was alive and hearty Jan. 15, 1885, and never used any tobacco or stimulents. He lived up to the laws of nature, and was always regular in his habits.

THE SMOKER'S CATARRH.

Habitual smokers, (says the *British Medical Journal,*) are notoriously liable to colds in the head, bronchitis and other congestive affections of the air passage. On this subject, Dr. J. F. Rumbold says in (*Hygiene of Catarrh*): "The congestion ocsioned by the action of tobacco on the mucous membrane of the superior portion of the respiratory tract resembles, in many respects, the congestion resulting from the effects of a cold. The local effect of tobacco on the mucous membrane of the nose, throat and ears is as predisposing to catarrhal disease as is inefficient and insufficient clothing in the case of females. The local effect of toacco on the mucous membrane of the superior portion of the respiratory tract, causes a more permanent relaxation and congestion than any known agent. As tobacco depresses the system while it is producing its pleasurable sensation, and as it prepares the mucous membrane (by causing a more permanent relaxation and congestion than any known agent) to take on catarrhal inflammation from even slight exposure to cold, it should require no further evidence to show that its use ought to be discontinued by every catarrhal patient. The only question remaining to be answered is, shall its use be discontinued at once, or shall the victim 'taper off' in his endeavor to become master of himself?"

The writer acknowledges but one successful method, viz. its discontinuance at once.

MOROCCO ON THE WARPATH.

In the Sunday Magazine of F. Leslie's of June 1887, it says: "The Sultan of Morocco has abolished the State tobacco monopoly. A regular crusade against it has been inagurated, tobacco and snuff shops have been closed, and large quantities have been burned publicly by the Sultan's order.

SNUFFING.

A lucky capture of Spanish galleons, laden with choice snuffs from Havana, had inaugurated the reign of Queen Annie, and been the means of introducing into England the Continental fashion of snuff-taking. Wagon-loads of the "titillating dust" thus imported being publicly sold at 3d. and 4d. a pound, the box soon rivaled and at length eclipsed the pipe. Sir Plume, "of amber snuff justly vain," became a character, and was kept in countenance as well by "the fair" at the drawing room as the Chairman in the streets. To parody a well-known line, "Snuff ruled the Court, the camp, the grove." Snuff-taking was elevated to the rank of a passion by the wits and beaux of society. To offer a box gracefully became an educational requirement, and a general flourish of snuff-boxes took place, if not "all over the land," as Cowper said, at least from Pall Mall to the 'Change. A pinch to conciliate, a pinch to contemn; a pinch gave pungency to the jest, a relish to sarcasm, and equally served to cover embarrassment and chagrin. Talleyrand used to say—and he was a *priseur*—that the snuff-box was essential to all great politicians, as time for thought in answering awkward questions was gained in taking, or pretending to take a pinch. Certainly prince Metternich was devoted to the box, and diplomatists generally appeared to have viewed it with favor, as well, indeed, they might, when some £8000 or £9000 were expanded in the purchase of boxes for presentation to foreign Ministers at the coronation of George IV.

SNUFF DIPPING.

The disgusting habit of snuff-dipping has spread among the female operatives in Massachusetts factories to an alarming extent. A year ago the Catholic Bishop of the State, publicly forbade this use of the weed, and for a time there was a considerable falling off in the sales of snuff, but the prohibition has now become practically a dead letter.

SMOKING IN HOLLAND.

The love the Dutch have for tobacco is well known. Nearly every man one meets in the streets has a cigar in his mouth; nor, unhappily is the habit confined to adults. Hundreds of juveniles are addicted to smoking, and they may be seen at almost any time enjoying the weed with all the nonchalance of grown-up men. Indeed, they often indulge in the habit in the company of their parents, who do not seem to attempt to discountenance a practice which in this country and in England has always been considered injurious to children, and the act itself, so far as they are concerned, highly unbecoming. It is amusing, but not agreeable, to be stopped in the street by an urchin four feet high, who exhibits the stump of a half-consumed cigar, and with unlimited assurance asks you for "en beetje vuur" (a little fire). Of course, unless you wish to be considered impolite, you must stoop to allow him to make use of the lighted end of your Havana, while all the time you may be doing great violence to your feelings.

The consumption of tobacco in Holland is enormous. There are some Dutchmen who smoke regularly from ten to twelve cigars each day. No wonder that in most of the streets the tobacconists' shops are neither few nor far between. In many of the principal offices smoking is going on all day, and tobacco would seeem to be as much a necessity in the counting-house as pens, ink, and paper.

The lower orders in Holland often smoke cigars which cost less than a cent each. Some may even be purchased at the rate of five or six for two cents, not cigars made of brown paper handay, or dried cabbage leaf, but real tobacco. The tobacco from which these are made is grown chiefly in the neighborhood of Utrecht.

It is stated that the plant was first cultivated in Holland in the year 1615. *Harper's Weekly.*

SMOKING IN RUSSIA.

The smoke which most forces itself upon the attention of travellers in Russia is not the smoke of the "peasant's towns." It is the smoke caused by the burning of tobacco in the debatable and much debated fashion pursued in the countries of Western Europe. Here, however, lack of power or want of will to smoke is well nigh unintelligible. A man who objects to smoking is a much more insufferable nuisance than the man who insists upon smoking. The Russians do not divide society into smokers and non-smokers; they decline to make railway carriages a sort of battle-ground for those who love the weed and those who do not; they refrain from suggesting, either by word or deed, that a man's social qualities or respectability can be at all correctly inferred from his attitude toward tobacco. The reason for this is that everybody smokes in Russia, and provision is made accordingly. Save the church, no place is here sacred from the weed. The papyros is no respector of

domestic sanctities. Every chamber of every well-
kept house has its pepeinitsa for the reception of
cigar ashes.   Hotels have similar conveniences,
smoking being practiced as well as permitted in
every accessible apartment in these buildings.   In
England the railway traveler is left to dispose of
his cigar ashes either by depositing them on the
floor of the compartment or by disposing of them
through the window.   In the former case the result
is always uncleanliness—in the latter the wind
sometimes interferes with the smokers project, not
always to the convenience of his fellow-passengers.
Here railway authorities provide a small box or
receptacle in each carriage for the use of those
who smoke.   The "tobacco question" is all the
more easy to deal with in Russia for the reason that
women smoke as well as men.   The Russians themselves—(I am here giving a masculine opinion of
the masculine sex)—are inclined to disparage fem-
inine indulgence in the weed and to regard the
women who smoke as socially "fast."   It is true
enough that one sees few women smoking in the
street.   Public use of tobacco in the daytime is
confined among the female sex to the peasant
classes.   At the same time disinclination to be considered "fast" is no proof of a woman's incapacity
to consume large quantities of tobacco.   As a matter of fact the middle and the upper classes in St.
Petersburg are all of them, with rare exceptions,
inveterate smokers.   The silver or gold papyros
case is much more indispensable than a fan to a

lady mixing in society. To be without cigars is to
be careless of one's reputation. For a guest lady
or gentleman, to decline a papyros, is one of the
most serious social offenses that can be com-
mitted.

THE SMOKING NUISANCE.

If a farmer can have choice between the man who
smokes and the one who does not he cannot afford
to hire the smoker. The smoker spends too much
time hunting for his pipe and tobacco and firing up
when at work, and though he pretends to smoke
and work at the same time the pipe takes most of
his attention, and the employer's interests suffer.
But more than this occurs—smoking makes a man
lazy. The first effect is to brace him up a little, but
a few moments later it relaxes his sinews, his energies flag, and he feels like crawling under the shade
and taking a nap. I know how it is, for I am an
occasional smoker myself. If I have business on
hand I postpone smoking, knowing by experience
that it unfits me for labor, mental or physical.

I did not realize how many times a day my men
smoked until I employed them in the office during
rainy weather. Some of them could not dispense
with smoking from the morning until the noon bell,
but wanted to indulge two or three times, feeling
uneasy under the restraint. I do not doubt these
men would smoke six or eight times daily in the
fields, and every smoke would entail the loss of ten
minutes, say one hour each day, or one day per

month—a loss of $12 for eight months. I assume that the risk of having a smoker about the premises is worth another $12 per eight months. No matter how careful the men may try to be, they are liable to lay the burning pipe or cigar down and forget it until the buildings are in flames, or drop a match in an absent-minded moment that costs the proprietor several thousand dollars.

Again I say I know how it is myself. I am one of the most cautious of men, and never enter a barn or shop with a lighted cigar, nor light one in the barn. One day, desiring to enter the barn, I laid my lighted cigar on a block two rods away, between the barns and a woodshed. Coming out of the barn I was met by some visitors and the cigar was forgotten. We walked down through the berry fields, and when we came back we found people fighting fire. The cigar had been blown off the block. It fell down among dry chips and litter, and we came near being burned out. Smoking is not only a foolish waste of time and money but a source of danger to property; it undermines health and unless the occasional devotee is scrupulously neat makes him less companionable. The inveterate, perpetual smoker is a nuisance.

The above article was written and printed by my namesake (whom I have never seen), Chas. A. Greene, the eminent Agriculturalist of Rochester, N. Y.

CRUSADE AGAINST CIGARETTES.   THE SUPERINTEN-
DENT OF THE NEWARK PUBLIC SCHOOLS
JOINS THE MOVEMENT.

TRENTON, Sept. 28.   The fight against cigarettes in this state has now assumed proportions
that make it especially noteworthy.   There has
certainly never been a more unique crusade.   Beginning as it did with the requests of a few business
men in the leading cities to know why the anti-
cigarette law of 1884 was not enforced, it has now
reached the grasp of the public school teachers,
who have taken it up with a vengeance.   The business men's movement is in self-defence.   They find
cigarettes unnerve and unfit boys in their employ
for work.   The teachers' movement is a purely beneficial one.   They want to stop a habit because
it is bad and destructive to health.

The leader in this latest movement is Superintendent Barringer, of the Newark public schools.   He
has sent notices to all the teachers of the state, requesting their aid.   In an interview with your correspondent, Mr. Barringer outlined the nature of
this work.   "The cigarette smoking habit," said
he, "has become so general among school boys that
there is scarcely one in a dozen over twelve years
of age that is not addicted to it.   Teachers all over
the state have done all they could to discourage
the habit, but without success.   We believe the only
way to put a stop to it, is to prosecute the sellers
of the paper-covered lung destroyers.   We propose

to proceed against both smokers and sellers. The boys can be suspended from school, and if they continue the practice they can be expelled. Nearly every candy store sells cigarettes, and the pennies parents give children for sponges, pencils, etc. are spent for cigarettes. The poorest quality of the article is sold. Physicians affirm that opium is largely used, and it is certain that the lung and throat troubles are produced by cigarette smoking."

LEPROSY FROM CHINESE CIGARETTES.

Leprosy, says a physician of San Francisco, has not a few victims among the whites. Especially is it revealing itself about the lips and tongues of boys who smoke cheap cigarettes made by Chinese lepers. The disease, though fatal, is slow in giving tokens of its first approaches. The doctor knows of one hundred and seventy cases, the majority largely Mongolian. The disease is highly contagious; sleeping in bed clothes handled by infected Chinese servants, even sitting on the chairs they have used, handling the same things, etc. is dangerous. The disease often is not observable for four or five years, and then only by physicians accustomed to examining such patients. In the Sandwich Islands, an island is set apart for lepers. The hospital has at this time eight hundred lepers, A vigilant eye is kept on the lookout for traces of incipient leprosy. When observed the person is at once sent to the hospital, but a great many are concealed by friends, and thus the disease spreads.

No case is discharged cured. One doctor claims to have counteracted recent developements by in-occulation. The leper does not suffer much pain until his fingers and toes drop off. When the leprous sores are still on their hands they work in Chinese cigar factories and give a wide spread to the infection. Clothes washer-men do the same.

ANOTHER CIGARETTE VICTIM.

TROY, N. Y. Dec, 28, 1887. Cigarette smoking numbers another victim in Richard H. Barringer, a popular young man of this city. He was a constant smoker. An affection of the heart was followed by dropsy. Several physicians attended him, and they all agreed that nicotine poisoning had so shattered his system that recovery was impossible. He is dead at the age of twenty-five years. Up to a few years ago he had a fine physique and was believed to have good prospects of long life. After his death one of his veins burst, and the blood therefrom was almost as black as ink.

DRIVEN CRAZY BY CIGARETTES.

[Detroit Special to Pittsburg Dispatch.]

During the past seventeen months an unusually large number of young men have been sent to the insane asylum in this state. It happens that nearly all of them were large consumers of cigarettes, and this fact has given rise to the report that cigarette smoking was the cause of their insanity. In several cases this is positively known to be the case, and there is consequently considerable alarm felt by parents for their cigarette-consuming sons.

INFATUATED WITH CIGARETTES. A BOY SELLS HIS SISTER'S BEDDING TO GET SMOKING MONEY.

NEW YORK, Nov. 25.—James Clarke, aged fourteen years, of No. 413 West Thirty-ninth street, was placed before the bar in Jefferson Market police court on complaint of his married sister, Mrs. Alice O'Brien, of No. 456 West Thirty-fifth street, who stated that the boy was a fit subject for some reformatory. Clarke's mother and father are both dead, and ever since his mother's death, (a few weeks ago,) he has, among other bad habits, become an inveterate cigarette smoker. To obtain money for this purpose he took the feather beds and pillows out of the house, that were worth $25, and sold them to a furniture dealer for $1.50.

A BOY FALLS VICTIM TO THE NOISOME CIGARETTE.

An eleven-year-old son of Joseph Seatham died at Tamaqua, Pa. suddenly on Saturday. Yesterday it was decided to hold a post mortem examination to ascertain the cause of death, for the boy had been in apparent good health up to a few moments of his death. The physicians decided that death was caused by enlargement of the heart, due to excessive cigarette smoking.

THE USE OF TOBACCO.

The first effect of tobacco when smoked is, that it depresses the heart's action, and this produces an irritated condition of this organ known as "tobacco heart." Another is that it retards development, and should therefore never be used by youths.

There is always going on in the body a system of waste and repair. The waste is carried away by the natural channels and perspiration. Those who chew, stimulate the salivary glands to such activity that some of the work of the kidneys is actually performed by these glands, a thought which, to say the least, is not pleasant.

Nicotine is a nearly colorless fluid which is reduced to crystals with difficulty. It has a strong odor of tobacco, a burning taste, and is extremely poisonous. A half-ounce of tobacco is said to contain enough nicotine to prove fatal. To be sure, smokers only get a small portion of this into their systems, but it is this poison which affects those who smoke to excess, or those who are growing, are nervous, or have a tendency to heart disease.

As a medicine, tobacco was used in former years to a considerable extent, but more recently it has fallen into disuse because of the large number of deaths resulting from its internal administration.

It is sometimes used as a remedy in poisoning by strychnine, as its action is directly opposed to that of strychnine, and it is also used in lockjaw.

For pc .soning by tobacco, alcohol is a good remedy, which is the reason men can smoke so much
while drinking alcoholic beverages. As a poison,
nicotine is so virulent that death ensues almost
instantly. A case is reported of a man who com-
mitted suicide by taking an unknown amount.
He fell immediately to the floor, sighed deeply, and
in three minutes was dead.

NOTE.

I cut the above article out of a newspaper. It
contains some valuable truths.

EFFECTS OF SMOKING.

A reporter of a New York paper recently interviewed Dr. W. A. Hammond on the effects of smoking, and he gave the result of his professional experience as follows:

"If children smoke cigars they destroy their nervous systems before they are fully formed, and
render themselves liable to neuralgia and various
functional diseases of the brain, which are certainly
calculated to destroy their mental force. There
is also evidence to show that tobacco in young
persons actually interferes with the development
of the body in regard to size—that it stunts their
physical system. It certainly impairs digestion
for they cannot use tobacco without spitting inor-
dinately. The saliva expelled from their bodies is
one of the most important of the digestive fluids
and the proper digestion of the food in the stomach

is materially interfered with when there is not
enough saliva left to mix with their food before it
is swallowed. Again, it certainly impairs hearing
and eyesight. I have seen several instances of
young children having their eyesight injured seriously, if not irreparably, by the use of tobacco.
The excessive use of tobacco is injurious to everybody, adults as well as infants, male as well as female.''

"Now as to cigarette-smoking. It is injurious to
everybody, practiced as it ordinarily is by inhaling
the smoke into the lungs. The use of cigarettes
has been increasing to a most extraordinary degree
in this country in the last ten years. I have already
seen the ill effects of it in my practice, in the production of facial neuralgia, insomnia, nervous dyspepsia, sciatica, and an indisposition to mental exer-
tion. In young persons all these afflictions are seen
with much greater intensity, and, consequently,
the effect upon them is very much worse than upon
adults. In France the difference between those
who smoked cigarettes in the polytechnic schools
and those who did not, as to their position in
their classes, was so great that the Government
has prohibited absolutely the use of tobacco in all
State schools. Some time ago I was consulted
by Commodore Foxhall Parker, then superintendent of the Naval Academy at Annapolis,
relative to the advisability of allowing the cadets
to smoke. He stated in his letter that it was almost
an impossibility to prohibit the practice, and put

the question whether it wasn't better to allow
them to smoke under regulations than to punish
them constantly for violation of rules. I replied
that it was a matter of discipline; but that, so
far as the effects of tobacco were concerned, I had
no hesitation in saying that its influences would
be injurious to the cadets, and that I had constant
evidence of it in my private observations otherwise.

WHAT SMOKERS USE.

A new fact has come to light connected with
cigarettes, that one would think would arrest the
growing practice of smoking, especially by women.
The finer sensibilities of women have hitherto been
sufficient to prevent the general use of tobacco in
any form by them. But there are women to-day
who use cigarettes, and the use tends to degredation altogether beyond what comes of being a slave
to the vile weed.

It is known that old cast-away cigar-stumps are
used in the manufacture of cigarettes. Boys are
employed to gather them from hotels, bar-rooms,
side-walks; from wherever they are thrown. Col-
lectors buy them of the boys and send them to the
manufactories by the barrel. No matter how disgusting the spot whence they are picked; whether
from the spittoon with its dangerous saliva, or the
gutter with its filth, the foul refuse finds its way
into the mouth and nostrils of the cigarette-
smoker.

But this is not all. Many a smoker throws away his cigar because he does not like the flavor of it. He does not know why the odor is unpleasant to him, but it is caused by nicotine — the active principle of tobacco, and a violent poison. This accumulates in the base of the cigar with every draught of the smoke, and the man, noticing the unpleasant smell, throws the stump away. This reservoir of nicotine finds its way into the cigarette, and the person who smokes it gets (in a condensed form,) the poison which works mischief on the brains of habitual smokers.

But even this is not the worst of it. These cigar-stumps have been in the mouths of all sorts of men —drunkards; fast young men; rotten old rogues, whose very kiss, or touch, or even the pencil they have held in their mouths might communicate the foulest and most fearful disease that comes to a human being. And yet cigarettes are smoked by men, women and boys.

UNPLEASANT OCCUPATION.

The States of New York and New Hampshire and Nebraska have made laws to keep boys from using tobacco. Of what earthly use are such laws, when the parents of the boys are all the time using the mouth-defiling substance and setting them such a bad example? It seems to me that (notwithstanding the fact that $600,000,000 worth of tobacco was used in the United States last year, and that all the counties in Pennsylvania, save six, are

growing the weed, and that $300 an acre is paid
in Lancaster county for ground to raise it, and it
is as common to see men smoke and chew, as it is
to see flies in mid-summer), that the avocation of
selling it in any form must be distasteful to a sen-
sitive, well-bred man. He knows that every inducement he makes by showy windows, or half-
column advertisements only induces young and
old men and boys to spend their money for a useless substance.

LIQUOR AND TOBACCO SELLERS.

No one engaged in the sale of intoxicants, and
tobacco can object to my statements. None of
them dare get up before the community and say, I
glory in my occupation, I thank God every day
that he has selected me for this avocation and that
he has given me health and strength to induce
(those who have large families dependent upon
their labor and who are sober) to drink rum or
chew tobacco, to teach young men and women,
boys and girls, the use of stimulants and how to
swallow brandy or gin, and how to destroy tobacco.

I am glad of my ability to pull them down to destruction, poverty, crime and death, to learn them
to reel drunken home to the worn-out, affrighted
wife, to strike, brutalize, crush and ruin her and
her family.

I am truly glad to see my patrons arrested and
imprisoned for crimes induced from the liquor I

sold them, to see them reduced from a good condition to poverty.

He cannot lay his head on his pillow at night and ask God's blessing on his day's work. He necessarily must be an atheist. For he is at war with mankind and never adds anything to their comfort.

POISONED BY HANDLING.

By all means avoid purchasing fruits, vegetables meats or any eatables from anyone who smokes or chews tobacco. His filthy nicotine covered hands will transmit the poison to anything he touches and the swallowing of the polluted fruits may cause a variety of afflictions.

THE TERMINATION.

In the foregoing pages I have introduced a bundle of statistics, incorporated with opinions and beliefs, which, as a whole, cannot fail (if read with an inquiring spirit) to satisfy anyone that tobacco has no business in your hands, pockets, or among your band of friends. It is a covert, insiduous disease and death-producing substance. Only the arch fiend could praise it and its works. Many of the facts are jumbled together. Something like a basket full of links of a gold chain, which, with a little care, can be made into a continuous ornament.

DRUGS IN TOBACCO.

Under the above heading on page eighty-nine, I refer to the immence business of making extracts to impregnate the tobacco to give it artificial smell, odor and color. If the subject was fully ventilated you would be horrified to know the character and quantity of the drugs thus used, and of their thus adding other ill effects to the poison of the nicotine. The most common smell which you perceive when a cigar is ignited is the extract of valerian. Wherever cigars are kept, in all boxes or cases, the odor of the valerian is apparent, and many stupids regard it as the peculiar odor of tobacco.

TOBACCO.

The effect of excessive tobacco using is two-fold —constitutional and local. It slows the circulation of the blood, blunts the nervous sensibility, and hardens and thickens the tissues of the body; locally it produces malignant ulcers. Of all the men who use tobacco, those who use it in order to quiet irritable nerves are in the greatest danger. They are on the high road to a complete break down of the nervous system—nervous prostration. Of the inmates of a certain asylum for the insane, seven-tenths of the males were excessive tobacco users.—Dr. Stickney in St. Louis Magazine.

IMPORTANT.

Hundreds of men, from some cause or other, stop the use of tobacco. supposing that they have done all that was necessary by thus abandoning the weed.   To such persons let me say, the ill effects never leave entirely the body, and especially the rear portions of the throat, except by proper medical assistance.   I have seen scores of cases of tobacco sore throats, twenty years after its final use.

HORRIBLE DEATH.

My friend (James B. Wiggin who resides at Cambridgeport and who keeps a store at No. 17 Bromfield St. Boston, and whom I have known for nearly a quarter of a century, learning that I was about to issue the Tobacco Slave, wrote out for me the terrible fate of one of his former companions.

"Dr. C. A. Greene, do you remember that watchman, that was on the premises where I was having my work done?   It was a curious case.   His name was Charlie Lauter.   When he came in to see me, he was always smoking.   You know that I am an amateur doctor; and I think I can "dognose" an ordinary case pretty well.   I told Charley he was smoking too much.

"Oh nonsense, tobacco never hurt anybody!"

Said I.   "Charley I can see that you are bringing real hard trouble on yourself by smoking."

"What form will it take?   Paralysis, liver-complaint or what?"

"I do not know; but if you do not stop, you will suffer."

He laughed, and said he would risk it. It was such a comfort to smoke in the long lonesome nights.

A month later Charlie did not feel well. Said he kind o' got cold, he guessed, his throat was hard and sore, and his tongue was stiff. He happened to go to the right doctor, a man eighty years old with no tobacco stains on him, with hair and beard white like silver, and flesh just fresh and clear as a baby—much like yours, Doc.

"Smoke a great deal, don't you?"

"Yes," said Charlie.

"Never hurt you, did it?"

"No; smoking never hurt anybody."

"I guess you will find it has hurt you" said the doctor.

"What is it?"

He hesitated and did not want to answer, but finally he asked the patient:

"Can you bear trouble?"

"Yes, doctor, what is it?"

Then he answered:

"I wish to tell you. It cannot be concealed much longer. You have what many are trying to get, 'a smoker's cancer.' "

"Will it kill me?"

"Yes."

"How long can I live?"

"You may live three, you may possibly live six months; you cannot live a year."

There, in a moment, was Charlie Lauter, under sentence of death for what 'never hurt anybody.'

I saw poor Charlie a week later. His cancer had broken through each cheek and under his chin, and under his tongue. It was an active, eating cancer. He was a kind, good man, fifty years old. He suffered dreadfully and had to have his hands tied to keep him from tearing his face open. He starved to death inside of six weeks. I have met many such cases. I consider tobacco a useless vice; a hundred per cent solid dirt and degredation, and the greatest enemy that the human race has to-day."

MY CONVICTIONS AND POSITION.

I hate tobacco in all its forms, as I do the arch fiend. I never had any inclination or desire to put it in my mouth, any more than I would a glass of sulphuric acid, and notwithstanding my dislike to it, I am compelled to see it and rebreathe the impure noxious fumes of men who, on the streets seem to take a diabolical pleasure in throwing out a volume of the concentrated nastiness just as you approach them from behind, on the sidewalks, in the city or in the country. No pure air anywhere only as you get away from smoking men. When the smoke escapes from a mouth full of decayed, tartarous teeth, with gums and tonsils ulcerated, swollen and inflamed, the fetid, malodorous breath is as unbearable as the exhalations from an old, neglected sewer.

CONCLUSION.

After many years of study of the above subjects, I say advisedly that it takes the major part of a year to get the nicotine out of the body, (after stopping its use) and cure the ill effects produced by swallowing the poison so continuously, and that the throat is the last portion of the system to get back to a normal condition.

Any further information on the subject matter will be cheerfully given by addressing the author.

FINIS.

And now, with all these accumulated statistics before the eyes of the immense concourse of people who are using tobacco, are there any excuses for its continuance? Yet such is the force of bad habits, and apathy sucked in with the nicotine, that you might as well expect to cleanse a filthy, mire-wallowing hog, without the aid of water, as to stop some humans from using the weed and killing, prematurely, their bodies.

C. A. GREENE, M. D.

No. 178 Tremont Street,

Boston, Mass.

Marvellous!

Mrs. Dr. E. W. Taylor of 658 Tremont Street, Boston (of the firm of Taylor & Colby), who has been a prominent practitioner for eighteen years, a regular graduate; understands how to administer drugs as well as any other M. D. in America; could not sleep more than one hour at a time for eight months; was in bed six long, long weary months; worst form of dyspepsia with complications; she had no appetite; horrible eructations; and thought herself at the end of life without any hope of recovery; exhausted her own and lots of other doctors' skill; suffered excrutiating pains. She was placed under Dr. Greene's charge on the 10th of April, 1889, *and on the 10 of May, she walked into his office and introduced herself;* been sleeping naturally.

MORAL: If the above statements are true, then you must come to the following conclusions : —

First: Mrs. Dr. Taylor had swallowed many indigestible drugs, which, instead of curing her, only increased her maladies, as they acted perniciously upon the membranes of the stomach and intestines.

Second: If she (a regular graduate) could not cure herself of dyspepsia and other afflictions, then she could not cure anyone else similarly diseased.

Third: If she possessed the same knowledge of the administrations of drugs as any other allopathic or homœopathic physician, then no other physician can cure dyspepsia.

Fourth : The quicker mankind understand the true condition of affairs, the sooner will all fraudulent practices die out, and Omnipathy will assume triumphantly her proper position, and revolutionize the practice of medicine throughout Christendom.

He does not visit any patients, but cures all the afflictions of the body by external applications (on the skin) of non-poisonous remedies. No deaths among his numerous patients from Dec. 4, 1888, to Sept. 4, 1889.

CATARRH cured for Fifty Cents. . Cure Quick for Catarrh sent (prepaid) by mail on receipt of Fifty Cents in stamps. *Consultation free.*

DR. C. A. GREENE,

178 Tremont Street   -   -   -   Boston, Mass.

A Physician, Surgeon, Oculist, and Aurist since 1849.

OMNIPATHIC COLLEGE.

In answer to the numerous inquiries of my former and present patients, and friends of the cause, let me say that I hope within two years to erect (on grounds in sight of the Unitarian Church in Arlington, Mass., of which I am a member) buildings for collegiate instruction of Omnipathic methods, and a Sanitarium where invalids may be speedily cured of their multitudinous afflictions with Omnipathic remedials.

C. A. GREENE, M.D.

OMNIPATHY ·

.

God never intended the human stomach to be a drug shop, but only as a receptacle for food and moisture, to be then converted into blood, and it is impossible to transform calomel, quinine, morphine or arsenic into this life principle. The above is Dr. Greene's conviction, after forty-seven years of medical practice as a student and physician. If you want to be converted, read his work of forty-four pages on OMNIPATHY. *Sent free to you.* Send your address.

Dr. Greene was a pupil in the Hawes School of South Boston, Mass. from 1831 to 1837. He has for forty-one years been trying to get money enough together to erect a college to teach OMNIPATHY, and in that way REVOLUTIONIZE the practice of medicine in the world.

He has for forty-one years, treated successfully all the multitudinous diseases of the body by external (on the skin) applications of non-poisonous remedies.

NO DRUGS IN THE STOMACH.

www.ingramcontent.com/pod-product-compliance
Lightning Source LLC
Chambersburg PA
CBHW032014010726
47493CB00007B/2393